Louise's Choice...

Thomas E. Berry, Ph.D.

WESTBOW
PRESS®
A DIVISION OF THOMAS NELSON
& ZONDERVAN

WestBow Press books may be ordered through booksellers or by contacting:

WestBow Press
A Division of Thomas Nelson & Zondervan
1663 Liberty Drive
Bloomington, IN 47403
www.westbowpress.com
1 (866) 928-1240

ISBN: 978-1-5127-7799-4 (sc)
ISBN: 978-1-5127-7800-7 (hc)
ISBN: 978-1-5127-7798-7 (e)

Library of Congress Control Number: 2017903559

Print information available on the last page.

WestBow Press rev. date: 03/22/2017

Contents

Chapter 1

While sorting his mail, Professor Jack Demonte noticed a strangely addressed envelope. His name was printed in large letters with red ink. He quickly opened it and read the printed message:

"Your sharia law article is your death warrant!"

Jack paused and wondered who was playing a trick on him. Then he remembered one of the ghastly murders the Islamic State in Iraq and Syria, or ISIS, had carried out in Washington, DC, and he shuddered. He immediately thought, *What should I do?* Yet his mind could not concentrate on answers; he was thinking of the consequences of such a threat. Death by ISIS could only be inhumane. He thought of Louise, his daughter, whose beauty was appreciated by anyone who came in contact with her. *ISIS could harm her!* He realized he was in serious trouble, but he could not think of any means of escape. The warning referred to his article that had just been published in the The *Standard*. The threat was immediate and he was open game for an assassin.

After a few minutes of contemplation, Jack quickly went to Louise's room and knocked on her door. She was in her bathroom and yelled, "Come in!" Jack entered as his daughter ran across her bedroom for a light robe. "Dad, you surprised me!"

"I'm sure I did, but I have some thoughts about your wanting to go to that institute in Switzerland."

Louise sat down on her bed. "Oh, Dad, I don't think much

about that anymore. It would be interesting for a summer but very expensive."

"I know, my dear. It's a bit awkward now, but I'm sure arrangements can be made."

"But why spend the money?"

"Well, I—"

"Dad, you're not telling me what you really want to say. You seem to be fearful of something. What's wrong?"

Jack gazed at the floor for a moment. Should he tell his daughter? It would only make her afraid, and that could affect her at school. Then again, perhaps she should know and be more careful. It was a terrible decision, yet it had to be made immediately. *What to do?* The answer seemed far away and unreachable. He went with his first inclination and said, "Louise, I just want you to be happy and find the hero of your daydreams. Surely you understand that?"

"Yes, Dad, but we've been through this so many times. Why are you bringing up the subject this morning?"

Again, Jack was caught off guard, and he almost told his daughter about the threat, but at the last moment, he hesitated and made light of his concern. Yet he knew he must desperately seek help in his situation. It would help him to have someone close. Since his wife had died in the last year, he had no one. Yet he did not want to place a burden on his daughter. In a rather awkward move, he waved good-bye and left her bedroom.

What was he to do? He could call the FBI, but since the time of the great election, that institution was no longer popular with the public. It had been weakened by evidence of fraud. The police, he felt, would be even more unreliable, because they were not trained detectives. Yet how could he stand up to ISIS alone?

Jack walked out into his garden. Looking at the mountains in the distance, he felt the sense of gratitude he always experienced when he glanced at the beauty beyond the hills of his property. He sat down on a white laced-metal lounge chair and enjoyed the view. Suddenly, a horrible thought came to mind: someone in the trees behind his fence could be aiming a rifle at him at that very moment. The sniper could have been waiting for his morning excursion through the garden. That would indicate that ISIS had been watching his movements for some time. They could already have chosen him for obliteration. The idea gave him another shiver.

He jumped up and looked deep into the darkness amid the large trees. No one was there. ISIS could have been, of course, but they had not caught him at the right moment. "Oh, what am I thinking?" he asked himself out loud. "I'm letting things get out of hand." Jack stopped for a moment and looked around him. He noticed the water buckets and decided he had better start his morning chore. He glanced over the flower beds and decided he would need to water the roots of certain flowers because of the draught that had set in the last few days. He began filling the water buckets. It was something to do, and it took his mind off his distress. The gardenias were blooming brightly, and the coleuses were reaching for the sun.

While busy emptying one water bucket after another, he suddenly thought of Roger Hamstead, the young man who had been courting Louise. He was a second-year student in law school and had always seemed erudite in making comments or judgments. He decided he would talk with Roger.

Back in the house, he casually asked Louise if her fiancé was visiting the next weekend. She replied in the affirmative and asked why he wanted to know.

"Oh, for no particular reason. I was thinking of talking with him about current politics. He always seems quite versant. I'm curious about his ideas."

Louise entered the kitchen and said, "I'm glad you like him, Dad. As a matter of fact, I was thinking of preparing dinner for the three of us this Saturday."

"Good. I'll talk with him while you do that."

The professor sat down and thought about the incredible note he had received. So far, he had avoided telling his daughter about the confusion in his mind. This was unusual, as he usually shared everything with her. Still, he preferred not to reveal his concern. Why should she worry, when he did not have a plan for confronting the threatening note? He began reminiscing about the lecture that had brought on such a menacing feeling. He could not remember anything in his talk about sharia law that was not already known and available in books and publications about Islam. He had not been abusive and had actually tried to be considerate in discussing aspects of sharia that seemed alien to Western culture. He concluded it would be wise to discuss the matter with his daughter's fiancé. Surely a student of law would have some insight into a proper approach to such a dilemma. Or was he just fumbling along, not really doing what should be done? He wasn't sure and felt even more uneasy.

Jack suddenly knocked over his cup of coffee as he was trying to pour more. Louise looked at him, astounded. His arm had had a sudden nervous quiver and caused the slippage. She had never seen him have such a motion. Quickly, she said, "Dad, do you feel all right?"

Jack said, "Oh, sure. That was nothing." Then he carried his cup into his study. When he sat down in his leather chair and looked out the window over his garden, he thought, *Wonder how it will come? Will they slit my throat or just shoot me?* He again cringed at the thought.

The threat from ISIS slowly took over Jack's thoughts. As he read the morning newspaper, everything reminded him of his ghastly situation. ISIS was usually mentioned in some regard on the first page, so he started reading the second. Events happening around the world just seemed to overwhelm him and made him much more aware of these events, and he was again reminded of his admonition. There seemed to be no escape.

He usually looked forward to sleeping in his room, but nightmares invaded his tranquility. When he dreamed that Marjorie Main was eating olives at his bedside, he awoke with a yell that scared him. He had not seen a film with that famous old movie star in many years and could not imagine having her in bed with him, eating anything. Fortunately, Louise was not at home when the old movie hag appeared in his slumber, but Jack was loath to even try to understand why such a strange occurrence could appear in his mind. The next morning, he called Dr. Evis Braster, his longtime physician and old friend.

At four o'clock, the doctor opened his door for his old companion. Jack walked back into the office with the doctor and immediately related why he was worried and substantiated his story with the note he had received: "Your sharia law article is your death warrant!"

Dr. Braster could not help but laugh. Then, when he looked at Jack and sensed the dread his friend was experiencing, his face took on a serious facade. Shaking his head, he said, "Jack, my first impulse was that it was a hoax, but when I looked at you, I understood what you are going through. I sensed the seriousness of the attack. There have been too many incidents in our country to find anything amusing on that note. Sit down, and let's talk."

Both men sat down in the leather chairs in the office, and Evis had his assistant prepare them cups of tea before she left for the day.

"Now, Jack, when did you receive this?" He held up the paper and looked at it under a desk lamp.

"Yesterday. And I haven't been comfortable since."

"That is understandable. Such things are too common these days, and they're developing a fear that could be an end to our country." Incidents from recent times flashed through the doctor's mind as he earnestly wished he could give good counsel to his friend. He recalled the killing of many patrons of a nightclub in Florida and then the Los Angeles murders of innocents at a party. Such horrors were now possible in his beloved country, and he was greatly disturbed that his friend was caught up in the hysteria developing throughout America. He knew that Jack had come to him for help, but he felt an ominous fear of any participation in such a debacle. Yet he knew he must take a stand and suddenly said aloud, "If we lose our ability to speak out and tell the truth, then we're lost." Evis sat back in his chair and gazed at the note. "You must do something!"

"But what? I've never carried a gun, and besides, they always track their victims until they can safely destroy them. The papers are full of such incidents, and the police are always looking for them!"

Evis slipped forward and hit Jack on a knee. "You must go to the FBI."

Jack squirmed a little. "But they've been so impaired since the election. Nobody trusts them now."

Evis sat back again. "No, I don't think so. Besides, they're all we've got. Well, maybe the CIA, but I think they stay away from individual domestic matters."

The old friends argued for some time, finished their tea, and separated with an understanding that Jack would approach the FBI and report back to his trustworthy companion.

Before going to bed that evening, Jack checked the security aspects of his home. The electrical system seemed in order, and the blue light was shining on the wall gauge. He typed in the family code, and the light turned red, assuring him that the house was secure. Finally, in his bedroom, he thought of looking under his bed but stopped and smiled. *I must be really going crazy! How could anyone be under my bed?* He stepped back from the bedcover and turned on a small lamp by his pillow. Then, without a thought, he fell to the floor and looked under the bed. *I am going nuts*, he decided after realizing what he had done spontaneously even though he had smirked at the idea. He sat down on the bed and thought of his situation. *It's getting to me, and I must be careful.*

After a restless night, Jack went down to the breakfast nook and found, to his surprise, coffee on the marble-topped table. Louise was singing softly in the kitchen. He called to her, and she came quickly.

"Yes, Dad? Relax! I'm up early for a change. Roger is coming this weekend, and I have a lot to do."

"Are the two of you staying here?"

Louise carried in a plate of fried bacon and eggs. Setting them down, she explained the plans she and her fiancé had made. They would be home for the evening. Then, on Saturday morning, they would drive up to the family's cabin near Deep Creek Lake. She invited her father to accompany them, but he refused. Louise had expected his refusal and became busy with preparations for the trip into the mountains.

In his study, Jack had a fretful afternoon. When Roger Hamstead finally arrived from law school, Jack immediately invited him into his hideaway for a conversation. The professor, already nervous from the threat he had received, brought up another subject that was bothering him. He asked Roger a straightforward question without any effort to bring up the matter carefully. "Roger, are you and Louise having problems?"

The guest hesitated to speak.

Jack continued. "I think you are. She's been very reluctant to talk much about you. I'm hoping that this weekend together will bring about some positive results."

Roger finally said, "We're just not sure about certain things, and we're putting on a brave front not to show our concern. I'd rather not go into detail, as we might be able to smooth things out in the mountain air. I will say that Louise would like for us to marry now and start a family. I really prefer to wait until I finish law school."

"Fine," Jack responded, willing to forego any more talk on the subject, but he added that he understood both sides of their argument. At that point, Louise interrupted the conversation by asking for Roger's help with some shopping. When she noticed that she had perturbed Jack, she quickly excused herself and told Roger to stay with her father. As she left, she again wondered what was bothering her dad. In her opinion, he was not acting normally, and his displeasure at letting Roger go shopping seemed to verify her thought.

After Louise's departure, Jack said, "Let's talk about you and Louise later. I have a very important matter to discuss."

"Oh?" Roger muttered, as if he didn't understand what more they would have to discuss.

Jack stood and took the folded note out of a drawer in his desk. "I want to hear more about you and Louise, but I've got something rather serious to discuss with you."

Surprised that Louise's father would be so abrupt, Roger sat back and watched as Jack unfolded and read the note aloud: "Your sharia law article is your death warrant!" When he finished reading, Jack turned to the visitor and said, "What do you think of that?"

Roger was silent, and his mouth was open, as if he were having difficulty understanding what he had just heard.

Jack said, "I have just received it, and I must say, it's making me fearful!"

After a pause, Roger sat up straight and asked, "Is this in reference to the article you wrote for the *Standard*?"

Jack nodded, adding, "Who would have thought it would be contagious? I merely outlined aspects of sharia law that can be found in any publication about that aspect of Islamic law. I said nothing new!"

"These days, you don't have to. Just mentioning sharia law is dangerous now."

"Has it really come to that?"

"Yes, and that's the problem. It's so bad that people are becoming distrustful. You can see fear in their eyes when the subject is even mentioned."

"What will it lead to?" Jack asked.

"Fear will rule, and we'll lose our freedom of speech."

Both men were silent for a few moments. "It will lead to anarchy," Jack surmised and asked, "Is it discussed much at your university?"

"Yes and no. If the subject comes up from some tragedy taking place in France or Los Angeles, then there is plenty of discussion. But as a subject for conversation, I believe people avoid it."

"What should I do?"

"Have you told your daughter?"

"Not yet. And that worries me greatly too. Should she know about it? I don't know. I fear that it will cause her great consternation."

"Yes, I believe it would. It has already made me feel strange. It's like being a caged animal. One can't get away from it."

Again, they were silent. Finally, Roger said, "After some thought, I believe you must tell Louise."

"Why? I believe she'd worry herself sick!"

"When I came this evening, she whispered to me that you were very upset over something. So she knows that something's amiss."

Jack was silent for a few moments and then, nodding, said, "I believe you're right. She should be on guard anyway. They might even kidnap her."

Just as they made their decision, Louise called them for dinner. As Roger and Jack entered the dining room, Jack revealed that he had decided to spend the weekend with the young ones in the mountains.

Louise's face immediately showed her surprise, and she said, "Why, Dad! That's wonderful. You never bother going with us. What changed your mind?"

"Oh, nothing in particular. I guess I just need a change of scenery."

The next morning, the trio left for the family cabin in the Allegheny Highlands, overlooking Deep Creek Lake. Once they had settled into their rooms, Jack walked out from his bedroom onto the balcony that overlooked the blue waters of the lake. He breathed in the fresh, cool air and looked with pleasure at the light blue sky hanging over the forest's tall trees all the way to the narrow beach. "What a glorious sight," he said to himself as he stood quietly gazing at the scenery.

Suddenly, the light changed to a shadow, and he looked above at a dark, threatening cloud coming from the mountains of West Virginia. He shuddered. It was as if the fear he had hoped to leave at his home had caught up with him, and he was again adrift in a sphere of hopelessness, not knowing which way to turn.

Fortunately, Roger and Louise came out of their bedrooms and stood on the balcony not far from Jack. They all commented on the approaching storm. Roger held Louise tightly in his embrace, and Jack, noticing the young couple's closeness, went downstairs to read the paper he had brought with him. It started raining when he sat down by the large stone fireplace in the cabin's hall, and he was soon joined by the others.

Louise asked the men what they would like for dinner that evening. "Should I fix something special for the occasion?"

Jack asked, "What occasion?"

"Nothing special! I just wondered how hungry you are."

Roger answered, "Louise, I don't think we are hungry right now. Jack, let's tell Louise about the note."

"What note?" Louise quickly asked, and then she added, "So there is something I don't know. Both of you have been acting a bit strange, and now I think I know why."

Roger laughed. "Louise dear, we've only been trying to protect you."

"What on earth do you mean?"

Jack took the note out of his pocket, opened it, and, in a rather uneven pitch, read it aloud. "Your sharia law article is your death warrant!"

Silence reigned for a few moments. Louise looked at Roger with consternation and then at Jack with fear in her eyes. "No!" she said, lengthening the *o*. "Oh, how horrible!"

"Yes, it is," Jack said, "and now you see why we were hesitant to let you know about it."

Louise stood quietly again, but her face showed that she was greatly disturbed. "It's a ghastly provocation."

"Exactly," Roger agreed. "Now we must figure out what we should do."

Jack answered immediately, "I've decided what to do. Monday morning, I am going to the FBI."

Roger said, "It seems to me that I've heard that the FBI has a special unit that investigates any evidence of harassment."

"Yes," Louise said. "At school, I've heard people talk about various investigations currently going on pertaining to ISIS."

Jack nodded. "I've heard that too. After all, what else is there for such a threat? One should go to the FBI, because they're the ones investigating ISIS."

"Odd, isn't it?" Louise commented. "The ISIS thing has caused so much worry. At least the FBI has agents working on it."

"It's all we've got," Roger said, and looking at Louise, he added, "And it's probably the best protection for you."

"Why do I need protection?"

Jack spoke up. "My darling girl, don't you realize that they could do something to you in order to harm me?"

"Yes, you could be kidnapped!" Roger said.

Again, the three were silent.

"Shall we go back to my question?" Louise suddenly asked. "What do you want for our dinner this evening?"

After a few suggestions, the three agreed on a spaghetti dish that was fast and light. The dinner, however, was a disaster. Everything reminded one of them about the threatening note, and the conversation was far from savory. They might as well have eaten beans from a can. No one was interested in food. Louise wondered if she should tell her friends about the warning, but Roger and Jack were certain that she should not mention it to anyone. Roger thought about his adviser in law school, but Jack argued that it would be best for him to tell no one. The trio settled down with coffee by the fireplace and reached a final agreement. They would wait to disclose any information about the note until after Jack had talked with the FBI.

That night, no one slept peacefully. Roger and Louise cuddled but found no interest in love. They got up and went out on the balcony for a while. Jack joined them there for a brief conversation, but it was in reference to the note and only added to their discomfort. The hoot of an owl in the forest was just mournful enough to give them all a shiver. "How can one sleep after that?" Jack asked.

"I can't," Roger confessed.

Louise, however, laughed. "I think we're all too nervous to sleep, and we're also probably overreacting. I don't know. I do know that I'm going back to bed and will not think about that blasted thing."

Louise returned to her bedroom and was quickly followed by Roger, who wanted to discuss the notorious note with her without her father participating. Before parting, they came to the conclusion that the professor was doing what needed to be done.

Later, Louise again walked out on the balcony and gazed at the darkening forest in the distance. It seemed quiet and peaceful. Many times in her youth, she had daydreamed about a marvelous hero on a splendid white horse coming to her through the forest.

It was a childhood fantasy, but it was still satisfying. She suddenly remembered her favorite poem and began reciting it to herself:

When Beauty and Beauty meet
All naked, fair to fair,
The earth is crying-sweet
And scattering-bright the air,
Eddying, dizzying, closing round,
With soft and drunken laughter;
Veiling all that may befall
After—after—

She paused and thought of her childhood fantasy. *Is Roger really the man I created in my dreams? No, he isn't. He's thinking of his career and money. He wants everything before we have the most important thing: a family.* She walked along the balcony and peered into her fiancé's room. He was sleeping peacefully. Somehow, she felt neglected. *He only thinks of himself. I'm just a link in his chain!* She walked back toward her room.

A sudden gust of wind closed Louise's door with a slight jolt, waking Roger. He quickly came out of his room and saw Louise in her doorway. "Darling," he called, "what are you doing up in the night?"

Louise went to her fiancé and put her arms around him. He held her tightly, and they embraced for a few moments. "I was just thinking of the beauty of our world up here in the mountains."

"Yes, it's lovely, but you should be sleeping. We have a long walk tomorrow if we take our favorite trail."

Louise agreed, and they soon returned to their rooms. Roger was asleep quickly, but Louise lay wondering. The ending of her favorite poem came to her: "Not the tears that fill the years—after, after."

Is that the way it will be? she asked herself, wondering about the married life she would have with Roger. After thinking about the future for a while, she finally fell asleep, asking herself, *What should I do?*

The next morning, Jack asked, "Were you correct? Did you not think any more about the note?"

Louise stuck her tongue out at him and laughed. It set the tone for the breakfast. When she served the country bacon, Roger asked, "Was it sliced Arabic style?"

Louise grabbed a hand towel and whipped it at her fiancé, who ducked and laughed. Jack smiled, but when Louise poured some milk for his oats, he asked, "Is it unadulterated goat's?"

As if to choke him, Louise laughed again and put her hands around his neck. Then she announced, "Listen, you two guys. I'm not going to be teased about this note business. I admit it can be funny, but somehow, I'm not laughing."

Roger corrected her. "But, darling, you were laughing!"

Louise looked at Roger and said, "Yes, I was, and I think it was good for me, but let's not try to overdo it. We are all aware of what we're up against, and it isn't funny."

"No, it isn't," Jack agreed. "So let's just have as quiet and peaceful a time as we possibly can while we're up here."

His comment set the mood. Louise suggested they have a picnic lunch on their boat. Roger said he would fish for a while. Jack reported that he would take a book to read. A plan was made.

Each tried to avoid even a thought of the note, but their effort was not completely successful. As the merry group made their way to the family boat, the professor told a story about Louise in a lighthearted manner. "Remember the time you slid all the way down this hill?" he asked Louise.

"Do you mean in the snow?" she said.

"No! And you know what I'm referring to!" Jack replied with a short laugh.

"Yes, I do," she said, "but you shouldn't embarrass me."

Jack laughed heartily, and Roger asked, "What happened?"

Louise answered, not giving her father a chance to go into many details. "I slipped on the mud on the trail and ended up ripping the back of her shorts and panties." She turned to her father and smiled. "Satisfied, Dad?"

Jack laughed again, and Louise continued. "Now that we've revealed a bit of nonsense, what about the time you put all the fish we caught into a bag that was open at the end?" She laughed.

Roger asked, "Did you lose your catch?"

Both Jack and Louise nodded as they said, "Yes!"

No matter what they tried, everything brought their thoughts back to their fearful situation. In the evening, after returning to the cabin, they all agreed that they would like to return home. They could not escape their situation; they would simply have to face problems as they arose. Monday morning, Louise went to school, Roger left for law school, and Jack went to the FBI.

The FBI headquarters' building on Pennsylvania Avenue was a daunting structure that would have intimidated anyone at the first encounter. Jack parked in a garage and walked to the stone building. Inside, he was asked if he had an appointment. No, he didn't, because he did not know whom he should see in regard to the problem that had brought him there. The clerk made a call, and an agent appeared. He introduced himself to Jack and escorted him into a side office. When Jack revealed that he had received a warning from ISIS, the atmosphere changed immediately. The agent went to the phone and made a call. When he hung up, he waved for Jack to follow him, and they went to an elevator, which took them up into the building. Soon Jack was surrounded by four men who were examining the note and asking questions.

"Mr. Demonte, we would like for you to tell us about the article you had published in the *Standard*. Do you remember writing anything that would have been offensive to Muslims?"

"No, I don't. I merely presented reasons why a devout Muslim could have conflicts with also being a loyal American."

"You feel that such a presentation would not be offensive?"

"If they accepted fact, then they could not believe that the article was provocative."

"Please give us an example of what you are saying."

"In the theological sense, no Muslim can be a good American, because he is obliged to swear allegiance only to the Islamic moon god, Allah."

"Were there other factors included in your article?"

"Yes, the social factor. Islam forbids a Muslim to be friends with other peoples, such as Christians and Jews."

"Did you mention any of the negative aspects of Islam?"

Jack looked at the agent as if he could hardly believe the question. Then he replied, "Heavens, what I've mentioned has hardly been positive. However, if you'd like more, I did inculcate in the article the Muslim treatment of their wives should they be disobedient."

"For instance?"

"Sharia law allows the husband to beat his wife under those circumstances."

At that point, one of the men interrupted the questioning. "Gentlemen, I believe we will be here all day if we continue this conversation. I think Mr. Demonte has given enough information about his article. He has shown that it is very erudite, and we must obtain a copy for each of us."

The other men agreed.

Jack was conducted to a studio where electrical equipment of every sort filled the shelves and tables. He was asked if he minded having more questions recorded. He didn't, and two of the men began arranging machines for such a session. When they finished, Jack was given a chair in front of a microphone, and the inquiries began.

"Mr. Demonte, would you mind telling us about yourself?"

"Not at all. I am sixty years old, and I have been a professor of world history with a theological concentration for twenty years at Johns Hopkins University. I have written several books that were published by noted university presses, and I have lectured at universities around the world. Since I am mainly interested in the theological aspects of a foreign culture, I have spent considerable time abroad. I lectured at the University of New Delhi when I spent a year doing research all over India under the auspices of the federal humanities. I have traveled extensively in Russia and lectured at several universities in various parts of that vast country. I also studied Islam when I spent

Louise a few questions before she left. Jack asked Louise if she could stay a few minutes, and she nodded.

"Miss Demonte," the leader said as they assembled around Louise, "do you have any fears about being followed by ISIS agents?"

Smiling kindly, she shook her head but added, "Of course, I'd be rather stupid if I did not think there could be some kind of harassment. They do harm family members."

An agent commented, "There certainly have been incidents, and that's our concern."

Another gentleman said, "You've noticed nothing of a suspicious nature recently?"

Louise shook her head, and the men excused her. Jack walked out onto the sidewalk with his daughter and asked the same sort of question. She assured her father that there had been nothing unusual. When Jack went back into the house, the agents had dispersed all over the structure. Each was carrying a pad and making notes. The leader, who was giving his men instructions, turned to Jack and said, "Louise is certainly a beautiful young lady. You've done well in single-handedly rearing her."

Jack thanked the bureau chief and asked if there was anything he should do to help the men with their investigation. Mr. Fermel said there would be a lot of questions once they had made the initial study, which Jack thought was taking an extraordinarily long time. When they finally did settle down for conversation, the first question startled the host: "Do you have a pet dog?"

Jack shook his head.

"It would be a very valuable means of protection to have a pet."

"Then I'll get one."

"We recommend a Labrador retriever."

"Why is that? It's not the type of dog I'm really fond of."

"What do you prefer?"

"I never had a German shepherd, but I've always admired them.

"That is also a good watch dog. I was merely recommending the Labrador because it is a strongly built dog of medium size and friendly nature. Yet they are also excellent guard dogs."

"I'll consider it."

"Perhaps your daughter would also be interested in helping yo decide."

"Probably so, but I doubt she will be living here very long. I think she and her fiancé are planning marriage this June."

Mr. Fermel was silent for a moment but then said, "Since she will be going away, I highly recommend you find a dog you like and can live with."

When the leader finished his inquiry about a dog, he called on the other agents to begin their questioning. One had studied thoroughly the electrical alarm system in the house and had found it well designed. He had a question about a dormer window in the side of the roof but accepted Jack's explanation that it was a sealed window and would have to be broken out by an intruder. However, the agent did mention a noted case in which a criminal cut into the wooden side of the outstretched window, avoiding the glass in case it would break. He then avoided the electrical alarm system and stole a considerable amount of jewelry.

A third agent asked if Jack had any problems with having some vegetation by certain windows removed. He explained that an intruder could easily hide behind a bush while his accomplice was entering a window. Jack said he would remove any plants or trees if it would help make the house safer. A final agent discussed the neighborhood. Was Jack in good standing with his neighbors? He answered, "Yes, with all but one."

"May I ask what the problem is?"

"There is a busybody across the street from my residence. She is not an evil person—that is, she is not nosy for contemptible purposes. She is just a terrible gossip. Well, we have a good relationship with her, but we are careful with what we say. That woman is capable of asking the most embarrassing questions. She'll inquire about a pimple on your nose or chin. She's just a sore spot on our fine street."

The agent was amused.

Concluding their investigation, the FBI agents told Jack what they expected to have happen in the near future. Mr. Fermel said,

"Since the note you received does not give any indication of when or where, we can assume that it is more of a warning than an immediate threat."

"Really?" Jack said.

"Yes. However, if you have any indication of further harassment, let us know at once."

"Certainly," Jack quickly replied.

"One last thing. If you would like for us to give you some help in selecting a dog, we could take you with us to a kennel that trains dogs for our investigations. You might find it very interesting. I don't mean to rush you, but as I said, we highly recommend your having a pet."

"Let's go," Jack kindly said. "I'm ready for anything."

At the kennel, Jack was soon enamored with a medium-sized Labrador that seemed to take to him immediately. He even suddenly called him David after a pet from his childhood. Mr. Fermel handed Jack a clipping about the breed. He read it quickly:

> General Appearance: The Labrador Retriever is a strongly built, medium-sized, short-coupled dog possessing a sound, athletic, well-balanced conformation that enables it to function as a retrieving gun dog. It has the substance and soundness to hunt waterfowl or upland game for long hours under difficult conditions; the character and quality to win in the show ring; and the temperament to be a family companion. Physical features and mental characteristics should denote a dog bred to perform as an efficient retriever of game, with a stable temperament suitable for a variety of pursuits beyond the hunting environment.

The director of the kennel suggested that they move on to another set of animals, but Jack bent down and hugged his new companion. There was no need to continue. Jack had his dog and seemed pleased. Mr. Fermel was elated that his effort had been so successful and fast.

The bond between Jack and David was even more evident when Mr. Fermel took them home. Louise was surprised that her father was so taken with a dog, but it did not take long for her to succumb to David's charms. Mr. Fermel left both father and daughter on the floor, playing with their new companion.

The evening was spent with each of the family members playing with the new pet alone or together. When it was time to retire, both members of the family wanted David on their bed. Jack persevered and went to bed with David cuddled up on his bedcover.

Jack felt content. Suddenly, his arms folded under his sheet, and his hands came together as if in prayer. "Dear God, I have taught world religious conceptions for many years, yet even now, I do not know how to approach you. When I think of the power and strength you offer to mankind, I am in awe. Yet I have deserted the Christian religion of my youth in my search for the meaning of life in the world's religions and philosophies. As a professor of theology who should know it all, I find that I know nothing. When I try to approach you, I do not sense with whom I am communicating. Are you the God of my youth? The Krishna I met in India? The Allah I served in the Middle East? Or are you from the philosophies of China? Even Buddha's 'no self, no problems' gives me no peace of mind. I have searched for you all my life, yet I cannot define you. And now that I have such a sense of contentment because of a mere dog that has befriended me, I am asking again for understanding. Dear God, I turn to you in need and in love. Please help me!"

Soon Jack drifted off to sleep. That night, he dreamed that he had slept with a dog. When he awakened, he was a bit confused because he remembered his wonderful new dog, but it wasn't on the bed. He went downstairs and found Louise playing with David. She said, "Oh, Dad, forgive me, but I coaxed him off your bed. He didn't want to leave you at first, but I begged."

"I'm just glad you like him so much."

"Oh, I do, Dad! I think he's just what we need."

"I guess I agree." Jack bent down and petted David as he asked, "Have you made coffee yet?"

"Yes. It's on the stove," Louise replied as she and David followed her father into the kitchen.

After the father and daughter had prepared their breakfast, he broke the silence by looking at Louise and saying, "Last night, I prayed for the first time in ages."

"Why, Dad, that's fine. You know I have a nightly ditty that you taught me many, many years ago. Remember?"

Jack nodded. "Yes, but my prayer was different. I prayed to God, not knowing which of the many gods heard me. You know that I have lectured about the religions of many lands."

"Did you mention Jesus?"

"No, because there again, I don't know which messenger of God I should address. Should it be Jesus? Or Muhammad? Or Shiva? Or Buddha?"

"Oh, Dad, you're too deep for me."

"Perhaps, but it is a dilemma. *N'est-ce pas?*"

"Not for me, Dad. You remind me of that Russian poet you sometimes quote: 'The Germen mind is so deep, he's fallen into it.'"

Jack laughed. "Funny that you should remember that."

Louise smiled. "The next time you pray, try Jesus. He's the one you sometimes quote in your talks on morality."

Jack laughed and opened his mouth to speak, but David ran to the door, barking. Jack followed him. Through a glass partition in the door, he noticed the weighty figure of Mrs. Shari Logan, his neighbor across the street. He opened the door, and her boisterous voice poured out from her broad, fleshy face. "Professor Demonte, I'm so sorry to bother you so early in the morning, but when I noticed the FBI agents at your door yesterday, I couldn't help but wonder if there was anything I could do to help you. You know, like good-neighbor character support?"

The troublesome and noisy neighbor was well known in the neighborhood for gossiping, so he was not surprised by her inquiry. He and other friends on his street had long ago decided it was best to just let her talk whenever she made it obvious that she was eager for scandal.   Jack smiled and withheld his laugh. "Won't you come in, Mrs. Logan? I believe there is some coffee available."

"Oh no, thank you, Professor," the guest said as she slipped into the entrance hall. "I can't stay but a minute."

"Well, do sit down," Jack said, and he pointed to a fancy bench in the hall.

"Oh, thank you again," she said, nodding as she took a seat. "You see, I've been so concerned about the families from that faraway place moving into our community. I just wondered if they came to talk with you about them."

"No, Mrs. Logan. They merely wanted a letter of recommendation for a former student of mine who has applied for government work. It was a vetting, you might say."

"Oh, I'm so glad it was nothing too serious. They stayed with you a long time, so it must have been a thorough investigation."

"It was," Jack replied.

"I'm sure you gave them the information they needed."

Jack nodded and then asked, "Mrs. Logan, have you heard anything unpleasant about the Syrians that have moved here?"

She raised her hands and beat the air down to heighten her comments. "Oh yes. I've been wondering why our police haven't done something about the things I've heard."

"And what have you heard?"

"Why, there's been thievery and harassment."

"Really?" Jack quickly asked, assuming that perhaps something pertaining to his own problem could come out of a conversation with her.

"Yes, the Browns have reported a stolen bicycle."

"Anything else?"

Mrs. Logan stuttered but changed the subject. "You know, Professor Demonte, it simply wasn't fair for the government to move all those people into our village with their strange clothes and habits. They didn't even ask us!"

"Yes, but remember, our fellow Americans voted this government into office, so in a way, they are receiving what they deserve."

Mrs. Logan frowned and said with a poised smile, "I think I do agree."

"Well, Mrs. Logan, I believe that only very minor problems have arisen from the Syrians moving to our midst, so let's hope it continues that way."

"I don't see how it can. The newspapers and news magazines have been full of things being done by unvetted people."

Jack paused for a moment and then said, "That's true, Mrs. Logan, so let us hope that it doesn't become worse."

"Or that it doesn't happen here," she said with a stern look.

"Yes," Jack agreed, and then he asked, "Are you sure you wouldn't like some coffee?"

Mrs. Logan stood up and said kindly as she walked toward the door, "Oh, forgive me for taking so much of your time."

"Not at all. It's always a pleasure to talk with you."

"How kind!" she sweetly replied, and she smiled as she tried to gracefully walk her weight out onto the porch.

Jack closed the door and stood for a few seconds in thought. "The old battle-ax next door is on the prowl again. I'll have to be careful around her."

Louise came down from her bedroom as Jack walked back to the kitchen. "I'm running late, Dad, so you can catch me up on the neighborhood gossip when I come home this afternoon."

Jack laughed. "She just wanted us to be part of the neighborhood news but was very disappointed when I told her that the FBI was here merely to get a letter of recommendation for a former student."

"That was very clever of you, Dad!"

"Her news will wait till you come home."

"Thanks," Louise whispered as she slipped by Jack, giving him a kiss before going out the front door.

Jack returned to his study with a cup of coffee and seated himself before the morning paper on his desk. There was unbelievable news. The president of the United States had approved the immigration of more than a hundred thousand Syrians, who would not be vetted by the FBI or Homeland Security. "What on earth is he thinking about?"

Jack asked himself, leaning back in his chair. "Is that wise?" He closed his eyes. "Nothing makes sense anymore. Why don't they see the danger they're bringing into the country? It's absurd!" Mumbling to himself, Jack soon fell asleep.

Later, the telephone ringing woke him. Startled, he grabbed the phone off his desk and coughed into the receiver. "Excuse me!" he said in a brusque voice. "Hello?"

"Jack, is that you?" a voice asked.

"Yes. Who's calling?"

"Mr. Temple, Louise's adviser at Loyola College."

"Yes! Hello, Mr. Temple."

"Is Louise at home?"

"No, she went to school."

"When?"

"This morning. Like she always does."

"Professor Demonte, I regret to tell you that she did not come to school this morning. We've been waiting for her at the graduation practice. You know that she's valedictorian and an essential part of the program."

"But she did leave for school this morning. I saw her off."

"There has to be some explanation."

"Just a second. Let me think." Jack paused briefly. "Mr. Temple, she always walks three blocks down the street and joins Sally Smothers. Sally has a car, and they've ridden to the college together for years."

Mr. Temple, in trying to solve the problem, blurted out some news that instantly upset Jack. "Yes, I know they come together, but Sally is here. She says that Louise did not come by this morning, and she did not have time to stop by your house."

Jack could hardly breathe. He seemed to freeze, horror stricken. Then he thought, *Could they possibly have done something to Louise?*

"Professor Demonte, I am concerned. What should we do?"

Jack stuttered and finally said, "I'm calling the police."

"Please let—"

Jack did not listen. The phone in his hand fell heavily on its stand. He then dialed the operator at 9ll. Once she answered, he could hardly talk. With great effort, he finally said, "Police!" When the call went through, Jack was still not able to express himself clearly. After several beginnings, he got only questions from a female agent. He hung up the phone and looked for his address book. When he found Mr. Fermel's number, he dialed the FBI. Fortunately, the head agent answered the phone. After a few minutes of conversation, Mr. Fermel understood enough to assure Jack that he was leaving his office to talk with him at his home. Almost in tears, Jack dropped the phone on its stand.

Sitting back in his chair, Jack said, "Christ Jesus, please help me!" Then, sitting up straight, he realized he had called on the Christian Jesus, whom he had not spoken to in prayer for many years. He was amazed and wondered aloud, "Why did I call on Christ? Why didn't I ask Muhammad or Shiva? What does it mean that I pleaded to the Lord of my youth?" He sat somewhat astounded.

After a few moments, his mind concentrated on Louise. She had left that morning, but evidently, she had not reached Sally's house, which was only three blocks away. What could possibly have happened in that brief time?

Suddenly, Jack felt David's chin on his leg. He reached down and petted the dog. "Yes, you know something's wrong, don't you, my boy?"

Captain Smith maintained that he had the legal power to attend such investigations. Mr. Fermel, evidently to avoid an argument, stated that he would be passing on any information he obtained to Homeland Security. The police captain took a seat without any rebuttal. At that point, Jack was at a loss. He smoothed the hair on David's back and finally pulled the big dog up onto his lap. He held David tightly, embracing and petting him. Jack was holding on to reality and thankful that David had come into his life. Part of his home was fine and safe. The other part—the space that Louise filled charmingly and beautifully—was absent. At least he had David.

The FBI arrived, followed by two police cars. In seconds, agents and officers were around and in the house. Evidently, the police had traced his phone number when Jack was too upset for speech.

Mr. Fermel, chief agent from the FBI, began questioning Jack about Louise. The captain of the police squad asked to be involved. It was then that Jack heard a conversation that caused him to be even more disturbed. The FBI agent reminded the police captain that the FBI was in charge of preventing terrorism and enhancing security in such situations. The police officer was almost in tears and had to be comforted by Mr. Fermel. After a few explanations about procedure, the FBI chief asked Jack to relate his version of what had happened with Louise.

Jack put David on the floor and sat up straight. "I am confused about this investigation, but I shall answer any questions you must ask." He sat back and began relating the telephone call from Mr. Temple at the college. He mentioned Sally Smothers and her relationship with Louise. He described the whole incident in simple terms and presented what he considered the answer to the problem. His daughter had been kidnapped while on the way to school.

Mr. Fermel reminded Captain Smith about the necessity for silence and reported that the kidnapping Professor Demonte had suggested had to be verified before the information would be given to the public. The police chief agreed and withdrew from the discussion. He then called his squadron of policemen and directed their exit from the scene. Then Mr. Fermel told Jack that he would contact Homeland Security since it was the government's analytical branch that focused on domestic security. The host was too overwhelmed for comment and sat back in his chair while agents continued their search throughout the house, especially in Louise's bedroom. Jack was continually questioned about small items in her room and became weary of having to repeat what he knew about certain aspects of the investigation. Had Louise ever complained about being followed? Had Louise ever mentioned anyone at her school making remarks about the Syrian immigrants now located in their city? Had Louise ever mentioned any problems with a schoolmate? Jack finally asked to be excused so he could use the bathroom. When he returned, the questions turned to Louise's relations with her boyfriend. Again, Jack was asked questions that he could not answer and informed the agents that they must ask Louise herself and that it was time to turn their attention to finding her. Mr. Fermel, evidently noticing that Jack was perturbed by his agents' inquiries, interrupted the session and informed the host that they would be in touch if further questioning was necessary. The FBI agents left, and Jack went to his room to rest.

Jack's mind could only think of Louise. He continually thought about her departure that morning and her usual walk to Sally's house. Surely someone would have noticed a kidnapping in the light of day? How was it done? Who would have dared? It could only have been ISIS, and the thought gave Jack nervous twinges in his face, right arm, and legs. He called David and let him rest on the bed with him. The dog snuggled close to his master, as if he sensed that Jack was greatly agitated. Yet there was no peace. After some minutes of stress, Jack heard Mrs. Logan's voice calling from the entrance hall. *Oh my God, what will I tell her?*

Jack crawled off his bed and went to the top of the stairs. Before he could discern how his neighbor had entered his house, he heard her yell, "They're announcing on the radio that Louise has been kidnapped! Is that true?"

Jack thought, *So much for privacy and secrecy*, remembering that Mr. Fermel had warned about exposing the supposition that his daughter had been kidnapped. In his nervous state, Jack went to the stairwell and shouted, "Yes, it's true! My wonderful Louise has been kidnapped!"

"By who?" Mrs. Logan called back from the entrance hall.

Her blatant grammatical mistake added to Jack's confusion for a few seconds. Finally, he loudly said, "We don't know."

"Was it—" She paused, as if afraid to speak. Then she added, "ISIS?"

"We don't know!" Jack repeated, and then he said in a rough voice, "Please, no more questions now. I'm tired."

"Oh yes! Professor, please pardon me. I'll rush away right now and see you later."

"Thank you, Mrs. Logan!" Jack barked, and he went to his bathroom. While there, he heard noises in the house, including the sounds of footsteps on the stairway. When he went out to check, he was greeted by FBI agents.

Mr. Fermel was already on the landing. "We are very sorry, Professor Demonte, that information was leaked to the press. We are investigating that mishap and have come to assure your safety."

"It's not my safety I'm worried about. It's my daughter's!"

"Of course, sir, we understand fully. Now we would like to discuss with you a plan. Shall we go down to your study?"

Jack followed the men downstairs and sat down at his desk. Mr. Fermel led the conversation. "We have been following the activities of certain members of the large group of immigrants from Syria who have been brought to our city recently. As you know, there are ten government housing units in the area allocated to them."

Jack interrupted with a question. "Is it true that they were allowed to come without any vetting? It seems impossible."

Mr. Fermel cleared his throat and looked around as if to inspect who was listening. "Such information has not been made public, but as you well know, it is almost impossible to silence the media. They have their own ways of obtaining info. I shall tell you, though, that it is true that all of those people were merely placed on planes and sent here."

Jack shook his head. "It doesn't make sense."

Mr. Fermel opened his mouth to make a statement but closed it and avoided making any comment. He then said, "Our major problem is language. We have an interpreter, but he is quite weak. Yet we are making do with him as much as possible."

"Is there anyone you suspect of harming Louise?"

"No, we do not know the people that well. We are still in the stage of early investigation." Mr. Fermel then added, "Please remember, Professor Demonte, that we do not know if your daughter has been taken by Muslim terrorists."

Jack nodded. "Yes, I know, but whom else can I suspect?"

At that moment, Mrs. Logan's voice called down the hall. "Professor Demonte, the mail has come, and there is a strange envelope with gobbledygook written on it!"

Mr. Fermel quickly sent an agent to retrieve the post. Everyone in the room was silent. Jack stood as if waiting to be assassinated. He was sure his blood pressure was rising, as he was experiencing fear he had never felt before. The agent returned with the mail, and Jack quickly grabbed it. A brown envelope stamped with large Arabic letters fell ahead of the rest. The professor quickly picked it up and nervously opened it. There was another note. Jack read it aloud:

LOUISE IS NOW UNDER SHARIA LAW

"Now do you doubt who kidnapped her?"

Chapter 2

During the month that followed the arrival of the second message from ISIS, Jack was a miserable human being. His raison d'être had been torn from him. He had lived most of his life in a scholarly search for the meaning of man's existence. When he'd retired from the university that had provided for his many trips abroad and his research in foreign capitals, he'd felt as if his search for meaning had been a failure. He had grown weary of his academic frustrations and, after the death of his wife, begun devoting more time to his daughter. Thanks to his devotion and encouragement, she had been successful. He was proud of having helped her develop into such a fine young woman. Now all that mattered had been taken from him by a cruel possibility. He was again without cause and meaning.

Jack tried various ways of escaping from the constant telephone inquiries and the questions everyone posed, especially his neighbor Mrs. Logan. The convoluted newspaper coverage of the incident led to rumors and misunderstandings Even Louise's fiancé seemed sometimes indifferent. Roger was evidently concerned about his fiancée, but he did not make much effort in helping in the investigation. Jack went to his mountain retreat but could not find solace. He returned a beaten man.

Mr. Fermel was greatly concerned about Jack's health and tried visiting him as often as possible. One afternoon, the host asked if there were any other kidnappings by ISIS in the FBI records. The chief replied in the negative; however, he revealed that there were

Jack quickly made a rebuttal. "But you're watching the airports. You must feel it's a possibility."

"I said that it was, but it's actually a remote one. We are just not taking any chances, as it could happen."

"Thank you."

Mr. Fermel paused for a moment and then asked the professor an off-topic personal question. "Mr. Demonte, can you think of anything in your daughter's character or in her upbringing that you would find unusual? That is, anything that would not be the usual desires or ambitions of a young, healthy American girl?"

Jack sat back in his chair and looked at the ceiling. He did not ponder long for an answer. "Well, to be quite frank and open about my beloved daughter, I must admit that at times, she seemed to be daydreaming about a sort of fantasy world in which she would like to partake. That sounds off, I'm sure, but she was always a romantic. Her dolls, for instance, would be given names from a sort of fanciful illusion. For instance, when she heard the Russian word *domvoi* during our travels in that country, she called a new cloth peasant-like doll by that name. It is actually a house spirit that can play tricks on its masters by hiding things in the house. She played with that doll for a long time."

Jack stopped speaking for a few seconds and then continued. "What I think I'm trying to show you is that she is very romantically inclined. Knowing that, I have been surprised that her fiancé is a rather conservative bore. They don't seem as suited for each other as I would like, yet she has accepted him. I don't know why."

Mr. Fermel commented, "That is very interesting. I am glad you told me about that aspect of her character."

The agent petted David again and then leaned back in his chair as he turned to another subject. "As you know, the FBI has created a broad base for its investigation. It is especially interested in the Syrian settlement that the government set up in our town. The ten small homes provided by federal assistance programs were mainly cooperating with the FBI. Only two families refused to answer questions, which brought on a tense and unpleasant relationship with the Syrians wanting to adjust to their new land. Of the families that did concur with the FBI, a Mr. and Mrs. Zafar were very appreciative of the attention given to them and most readily participated in any inquiries. We are hoping to establish a close relationship with this family as a means of learning the topics and interests of these immigrants."

Jack found the FBI's investigation of the immigrants a positive move and related his feelings to Mr. Fermel. After another discussion about the matter, Mr. Fermel departed, feeling much better about Jack's mood and attitude.

One day soon after their conversation about Louise, Jack was playing with David in the yard of the Demonte home, when Mr. Fermel came and mentioned that he had some news. The host immediately invited the agent into his home and offered coffee or a drink as they settled in the study. Mr. Fermel had no news about Louise, which was a great disappointment for Jack, but he did have an interesting proposition. The chief of the search for Louise offered Jack a chance to participate in the activities of a Syrian home.

"Professor Demonte," Mr. Fermel said, "the FBI has been able to develop a proper and timely relationship with one of the Syrian homes. Mr. and Mrs. Zafar have been most willing to share information about themselves and others in the small settlement. They also speak English."

"Has there been any news of Louise?" Jack said.

"Nothing has arisen that will give you some contentment, I am sorry to say."

"What could there be?" Jack asked, grabbing at straws.

"Professor, we are well aware of the anguish you are suffering. You, of all people, know the Muslim religion and its major premises better than anyone. Your years of scholarly research are an invaluable resource for us and the world. However, while we know the great amount of time you have spent in the Middle East, we think the project we want to propose would be of help to you."

"What are you referring to?"

"Mr. and Mrs. Zafar greatly sympathize with your distress over the kidnapping of your daughter. They wonder if it would help you to visit with them and observe some of the habits of a Syrian home."

Jack shook his head.

"Please allow me to explain the situation in more detail. They believe their knowledge of what your daughter might be experiencing would be of interest to you."

Jack paused and looked up at Mr. Fermel. Finally, he said, "If you feel it would be of a beneficial nature for me, I'll gladly accept."

Mr. Fermel sighed and sat back in his chair. "I thank you most sincerely, Professor Demonte. May I take you to meet them this afternoon?"

The government housing for the Syrian immigrants consisted of ten small houses in a row on open land near the city park. Mr. Fermel drove Jack to the scene and stopped in front of the third modest structure. They did not depart the car immediately, as they watched two small boys playing on the lawn with cotton bags. One boy was hopping in a bag and jumping as far as he could without falling. Once he fell down, the other boy tried outdoing the distance. Jack was amused.

The parents of the children, Mr. and Mrs. Anas Zafar, soon came out of the house and stood in front. Mr. Fermel invited Jack to meet them. As they approached, Mr. Fermel whispered to his companion that the titles of Mr. and Mrs. were always used in Arabic society with only the first names of Arabs. Jack thanked him as they reached the couple. Mr. Fermel held out his hand to Mr. Anas, who smiled kindly and shook hands with both visitors. Then he introduced his wife, Badra, and led them into the parlor, which was sparsely furnished.

"Gentlemen," Mr. Anas said, and he bowed his head. Then, as he pointed to the few straight-backed chairs in the room, he added, "Won't you please take a seat?"

As they seated themselves, Jack could not wait and asked, "Is there a chance that you know something about my daughter?"

Mr. Anas frowned and said, "Professor Demonte, I and my family are Muslims who would never ever participate in such a monstrous act. We want you to know that we sympathize fully with you."

Mrs. Anas, to the surprise of Mr. Fermel and Jack, spoke out. "Yes, we are Muslims, but we have modern perspectives of the Koran."

"My wife wishes to say that like most educated Muslims, we know that our religion, like all religions, has trends that give different perspectives to the Koran."

Jack asked, "Do you mean to say that you do not beat your wife, as the Koran allows?"

"That's correct. While the wife is subservient to her husband, I believe that he must treat her with respect and love."

Jack said, "Then tell me—do you think that my daughter has been made to marry an Arab?"

Mrs. Badra stood and stepped behind her husband, letting him reply.

"We could not possibly answer that question. Such a situation has not happened before. However, if you were Muslim, it could be possible that your daughter has been forced to marry."

Jack took out a handkerchief and wiped the tears forming in his eyes.

Mr. Fermel asked the couple if they had any children.

They nodded together, and Mr. Anas said, "Yes, our two little ones up front playing and a son, Mr. Daoud, who is finishing college."

The agent asked, "What is Mr. Daoud studying?"

Mr. Anas shook his head and looked sort of downcast. "He has been in engineering, but a friend, Mr. Amir, is visiting from Iran and influencing him in changing his program."

"You seem not to be pleased with the possibility of his going into other studies."

Mr. Anas sort of squirmed, as if he did not know how he should react. Finally, he said, "It's just a personal thing. He'll be all right, we're sure."

Mr. Fermel nodded as he agreed and apologized for asking something that was a bit displeasing.

"Oh no, no, no!" Mr. Anas quickly spoke up. "It's really nothing serious and will be worked out shortly, we're sure."

Mrs. Badra nodded her agreement.

After further conversation about contrasts in the Muslim and Western living styles, Mr. Fermel noticed that Jack was weary, and he made excuses for leaving. When they departed, the Anas family asked them to return, and Jack nodded his approval.

So began another month of waiting. At first, Jack looked forward to daily reports from the FBI. Other times, he merely sat and reminisced about the many travels he had made during his lifetime. He had visited every continent and so many countries that he had lost count. Certain places appealed greatly to him, and he often thought of returning to a few of them. He was especially fond of recalling the beauty of Lake Bled in Slovenia, at the foot of the Alps. It seemed that only Walt Disney could have created it. The small lake reflecting the mountains had many aspects of romanticism. There was a reined castle on a high bluff, there was an ancient church on a small island in the middle of the water, and it was all surrounded by beautiful forests and flowers. How often he and his wife had walked around the natural paradise while Louise played and skipped in front of them. His longing for those moments of long ago was soon replaced by David's pulling on one of his trouser legs for their daily outing. His life had become centered on David. They walked, talked, and sympathized with each other constantly. David's strength revitalized Jack's. A daily routine had been established, and it seemed to all that they were somewhat content. Then, finally, the post brought another message. This time, it was more than shocking; it was unbelievable.

The letter read, "Dad, I am married and very happy. Allah is king."

Jack sat back in his soft chair as if hit by a lightning bolt. His mouth opened as if he needed air, and he crossed himself, saying, "She's alive!"

Upon notification of the message, Mr. Fermel was soon at the Demonte residence, talking with Jack. "This is simply unheard of in the annals of ISIS terror, but it does give us much information for our investigation. However"—Mr. Fermel paused and looked seriously at Jack—"I must ask you if you can believe the message. That is, knowing your daughter as you do, can you see anything foreign or forced in the message? Can you believe her?"

"Yes, I can. She called me Dad, as she always has, and she would not lie to me about something so serious."

"What about the allegiance to Allah?"

"That is not as unusual as one might think. You must remember that I have searched the world's religions and philosophies for the meaning of life. Louise was always a good listener and practically followed my studies. We always considered ourselves Christians, but we did not attend church and found meaning in all men's faiths." Jack hesitated for a second and then added, "We even found consolation in nature."

"A very worldly view, I would say," Mr. Fermel commented.

"It's the view of the present pope, Pope Francis. He stated that for many men, nature can be a church."

"I think you've made me understand your daughter's situation very much. Perhaps she was introduced to Islam in an intellectual manner and could understand its precepts easier than the average American girl. Being reared in your home, with your studies covering such a wide variety, she certainly had advantages not given to many."

Jack sat up and thanked Mr. Fermel for his understanding of why it would have been possible for Louise to accept Islam. "However," Jack added, "the only thing that bothers me is the fact that she evidently married. Whom did she marry? She was engaged to be married to a young man in law school. It's true that I doubted their sincerity, but how could she change her mind so abruptly?"

Mr. Fermel did not answer and only shook his head. Finally, he said, "That's a question I simply cannot answer."

Jack continued. "You see, in my studies of Islam, I have noticed that Muslim men highly praise virginity. I hesitate to comment about such a thing, but I do believe that Louise and Philip never had sexual relations. You know how young people are today. Nothing seems to bother them. That is, it seems that conventions just don't matter. Louise, however, has a strong character."

"Do you know for sure that they never had conjugal relations?"

Jack nodded and then related what he knew. At their summer place in the mountains, his daughter and her fiancé slept in separate rooms. Louise's boyfriend wanted them to be together, but she knew that her father did not approve of such an arrangement, so she simply refused.

Mr. Fermel nodded his agreement, and the two men gave David some attention for a few minutes. The dog jumped and ran from one to the other. Finally, the FBI agent said, "Professor Demonte, you surprise me."

"How so?"

"I expected you to be in tears when I arrived, but you seem to have accepted the message merely because you felt that Louise was alive."

"It's true, because that was the important thing."

"I agree, and now we must find her."

To Mr. Fermel's surprise, Jack abruptly said, "I'm not so sure."

Mr. Fermel's forehead wrinkled as he gazed down at Jack in disbelief. "You don't want us to find her?"

"I'm not sure that it would be a good idea now."

"Why?"

"My daughter says that she is content. She might be harmed if your agents storm a mosque where she is being kept."

"Yet surely you want her freed from the people who kidnapped her."

"Yes, but she gives no indication that she has been harmed. Besides, I know that she will come to me when there is no possibility of her causing her captors trouble."

"Goodness!" Mr. Fermel called out as he ran his hand through his hair and looked heavenward.

Jack smiled and said, "I will rest peacefully from now on, knowing that she is content."

"But surely you realize that they might have forced her to write such a note. They may even have written it themselves."

"I just can't believe that," Jack replied, and both men were silent for a few moments. Finally, Jack asked, "Where will you look for her?"

Mr. Fermel sat down across from the professor. "We believe she is being held in a mosque here in America."

"Are there so many?"

"According to the Global Muslim Community reporting on IslamiCity.com, there are over two thousand in our country."

"That seems impossible."

Nodding, Mr. Fermel said, "So you see, we have a terrific task ahead. We have no clue as to where they have taken Louise."

"Maybe she's not in a mosque."

"There is also that possibility."

After a few moments of reflection, the professor asked that the FBI wait for another message from his daughter. "You see, Mr. Fermel, I am sure that Louise would be trying to communicate with me if she were in a dire situation. She does not seem to be. Therefore, I ask that you have patience for a while."

Mr. Fermel laughed. "This is certainly a change of scope, is it not? Usually, we are forced into action by people wanting justice immediately. You are just the opposite. You want us to slow down. I cannot help but find that amusing."

Jack smiled. "Do you agree then?"

"Not completely, but we're willing to give your plan a trial. We have things in process that will continue, but we shall hope you receive news that can help bring this rather unusual situation to a close. It's sort of like having the guilty solve his own crime."

Jack laughed.

Before his departure, Mr. Fermel commented, "I am glad I am leaving you in such a great frame of mind. I was worried about you. Now I'm not."

Again, the days of waiting began. Jack and David revived their routine, and everything seemed to be fine. Jack spent his time reading and watching world news, which was one of his greatest interests. Only one thing disturbed him in his daily activity: once Roger, Louise's fiancé, learned about the message from the captive, he seemed to just disappear. Not once did he call Jack for any information about his bride-to-be, and Jack was disappointed in him.

A particular thought often came to the professor's mind.

He knows she is honestly reporting her situation, but he seems to be dropping their relationship without any justification that she is definitely married. There must not have been much relevance in their marriage plan. Perhaps he considers himself fortunate that Louise has broken their engagement? They certainly had disagreements. He was pulling them in one direction, and she was pulling in another. He must think that their discord has been settled by her present situation. His silence would make one think that he is now out of the picture. You'd think he would be eager for news about his fiancée, but he certainly doesn't show any interest. Perhaps Louise is fortunate.

That idea strengthened with time. Yet most of Jack's thought pertained to the present. What was Louise doing, and where was she?

Mr. Fermel kept Jack informed of any information he could relay, but their talks became further apart. Finally, two months after their last meeting, the FBI agent called and said he had some information of great interest for Jack and suggested they meet that afternoon. They did.

When Mr. Fermel entered the Demonte residence, Jack could tell by the expression on his visitor's face that he had some pleasant news. After they seated themselves in the study, the agent smiled and said, "We've heard from her!"

"Oh." Jack sighed and fell back in his leather chair. "She's well?"

"Yes, but things are much more complicated than we realized."

"What do you mean?"

"She wants to bring her husband to you for a visit."

"That's wonderful!"

"Yes, I suppose it is, but what a complicated situation. She's supposed to be a victim of kidnapping, but was she?"

"What do you mean?"

"In the history of the FBI, there's never been a kidnapped victim who wanted a visit away from her kidnappers or a kidnapped victim who wanted to present a kidnapper as a friend."

"But …" Jack could hardly talk. Nothing made sense.

Mr. Fermel leaned over the desk and said, "Professor, your daughter wants assurance that there will be no arrests if she and her husband come out of wherever they are being held. It leaves us in an unusual situation. If he is an American and they are married, we could not arrest them. If they aren't married, then we have to arrest them."

"But she says they are married."

"Is that under sharia law or US federal?"

After a slight pause, Jack pleaded, "Oh, Mr. Fermel, let them come to me for a visit. You'll be kept in charge. I can see to that!"

"I believe you, but it's complicated. If they suddenly appear and are married, I'd have no right to arrest them. We know nothing about her disappearance and have assumed that it was a kidnapping. We could appear rather hasty if they were legally married."

"Why don't you let them come?" Jack pleaded. "And how can you notify them to come?"

"We're to print a welcome in a particular paper."

"I'll be glad to pay for it!" Jack interjected, and Mr. Fermel laughed.

One afternoon a week later, Jack was playing with David in the back garden, when he heard a familiar voice calling out, "Dad! Dad!" He looked up at the patio and saw Louise waving. Her eyes made contact with his, and she ran down the flower-lined steps to the garden. As she ran, she passed a tall dark-haired man Jack assumed was her husband. Louise quickly reached her father and enfolded him in her arms. Crying, she said, "Oh, Dad, will you ever forgive me?"

"Nonsense!" he whispered, and he kissed her cheeks. By the time they had quit crying and clutching each other tightly, the handsome man had left the patio and joined them.

"Dad," Louise said, pulling the man toward them, "please meet Daoud Faisal, my husband."

The two men smiled as they looked at each other and shook hands. Jack was impressed by the muscular figure before him and said, "Welcome to our home."

Daoud answered in perfect English and expressed his relief at being welcomed so readily and kindly by his wife's father. Louise said, "Dad, we are here for only a short visit. We are under arrest by the FBI and have to return to the place where they are holding us."

"Why?" Jack asked, alarmed.

"We were married under sharia law, and that is not a legal affair here in our country."

"In England, they allow it."

"It's a matter of time," Daoud said, putting his arm around Louise.

Louise continued. "Mr. Fermel is waiting for us outside in his car. He's been very kind and evidently likes you very much."

Jack smiled. "Yes, we've spent quite a bit of time together since you disappeared. But tell me now, as I have been eager to know—did masked ISIS terrorists kidnap you?"

Louise and Daoud both laughed.

"No, Dad, it wasn't like that at all."

Daoud spoke up. "Well, it was, and it wasn't."

"What do you mean?" Jack asked.

"I told the FBI that I got into the car by my own volition," Louise said. "I implied that I knew Daoud."

"Why did you do that?"

"So he wouldn't be accused of being a kidnapper."

"But he was, wasn't he?" Jack asked, almost scared at the lie being told.

"Yes, but it was like this. A black limousine pulled up to the curb, and a man asked me for directions. I didn't understand and walked over to the car. When he opened the door, I saw a gun. I was frightened and entered the car."

"But then it was kidnapping, and the story about hooded men grabbing you was just a rumor."

Louise shook her head. "Dad, I have to say it wasn't kidnapping, or Daoud will be charged with a crime."

"How can that be avoided?"

"The lawyers of the FBI are trying to establish cause for such an arrest. You see, I'll say that there was no kidnapping and that Daoud and I were married under sharia law. Where to place blame or whatever is the problem for them to figure out."

"But you were kidnapped!"

"Yes, but you don't know yet what really happened."

Jack stepped back and looked at his daughter. "Louise, you

must explain to me what did happen, because I lived through heck worrying about you."

"I'm so sorry, Dad, but I know you'll forgive me."

The professor paused and then said, "Let's go up on the patio and have a drink while you reveal this mystery."

The young couple agreed and followed Jack up the garden walk and staircase. The professor commented as they mounted the steps, "My nasturtiums never bloomed so brightly. It must be because you're home."

"Oh, Dad, how kind!"

Once the group was seated around a glass-topped patio table and had drinks—Jack a beer and the young people lemonade—Louise revealed the events of the day of her disappearance.

"When I slipped into the limousine, I knew immediately that I was not in danger. The gun was no longer in view. I sat in the back with Daoud, and he could not have been kinder. Frankly, I was impressed from the beginning by his stalwart and handsome appearance."

"Thank you, darling," Daoud interjected.

Jack immediately said, "But you were there to kidnap her! Why?"

"I shall confess to you that I was a member of an underground organization that sought to punish you for your criticism of sharia law."

Jack protested immediately. "But there was no criticism in my article!"

"We felt otherwise."

Louise broke into the conversation. "Dad, I was not mistreated in any way. I cannot say where we went, but I was given comfortable quarters and an explanation of why I had been taken."

"Why was that?" Jack asked at once.

"To punish you, of course," she answered.

"They certainly achieved their goal."

Daoud and Louise smirked. "I'm so sorry, Dad!"

"There's something about this story you're telling me that doesn't quite make sense. I can't quite figure out what it is, but it seems that there are several loose ends that you're not explaining."

"Yes, I'm sure," Daoud responded. "You are concerned about the underground group that sponsored the kidnapping. Naturally, we have not confessed anything about it. The FBI has tried tricking us into revealing its existence so that they can arrest me. Since Louise is instrumental in helping me deceive them, we have no reason to fear detainment much longer."

Jack turned to his daughter. "But, Louise, you are helping with a criminal injustice. Daoud and his group are breaking our laws. How can you do this?"

"Dad, I fell in love with Daoud, and I would do anything to help him."

"Even deceive your own country?"

"But, Dad, it isn't that serious. I'm not deceiving my country. I am just thankful that I am an American and live in a country where I have the right to arrange my future. I was not harmed, and you were not harmed. There is no guilt if we just leave the organization in the realm of the unknown."

Jack shook his head as if in shame. "Oh, what pretty language you are using, but for such a despicable cause."

"Dad, it isn't. If we just keep it secret, there's no crime involved."

"Is it possible that you, brilliant as you are, would disown honesty and righteousness for the sake of—" He couldn't finish his sentence.

At that moment, Mr. Fermel came out onto the patio and announced that they must return to FBI headquarters. They had stayed past the allotted time for the visit.

Jack asked the agent if the couple could stay a little longer, but he refused. However, he remarked that they would have free time the next day.

The professor walked over to his daughter and said, "We shall discuss this further tomorrow. I hope you understand."

They all agreed and dispersed.

A short time later, Mr. Fermel returned, and David barked his approval. When Jack came to the door, he readily allowed the agent to enter, asking, "Is something wrong?"

"Only you can tell me that, Professor."

"What do you mean?"

"I think you know. Shall we sit down and discuss it?"

Jack and David led the guest into the study. Once seated, Mr. Fermel came right to the point. "Dr. Demonte, we believe that your son-in-law is involved in very dangerous activity with an ISIS cell."

Jack shook his head. "Oh no! Surely not!"

"Yes, and we arranged the meeting you had with him today so that you might be able to help us in the investigation."

Jack's forehead wrinkled. "How can I do that?"

"We feel that you have learned something we would like to know. Will you cooperate with us in carrying our investigation to fruition?"

Jack bowed his head but said nothing.

"I know that we are asking very much of you, but we also know that you are a man with a noble and honest character. We must know the truth about your daughter's husband and the cell that we believe he is operating in."

Almost in tears, Jack sighed and sat back in his chair to wipe his eyes. Finally, when he had control of himself, he slowly said, "Mr. Fermel, I must have time to consider many things. I want to help you, and I am sure I will, but please give me some time."

Mr. Fermel nodded. "That's exactly what we are doing. This first meeting was the beginning of our plan. I mentioned that they could visit you tomorrow. We are holding them under the pretense of waiting for a court's decision about their marriage. So you will have them every day until we are confident that our suspicions are either correct or wrong. In a sense, you will be working with us, and we shall be most thankful for your support."

Jack stood and said, "Then I am to pretend that all is well and that I assume they will be freed very soon."

"Yes, that is what we are asking of you until we are content with the outcome."

Jack mumbled, "God be with us."

Mr. Fermel stood and prepared to leave.

Jack asked, "Where are the young folks staying?"

"Professor Demonte, I cannot divulge that, and I'm sure you

understand why. However, I can tell you that they are in very spacious and fine quarters. So fine, in fact, that I'm sure they think they'll be released very soon. Let's hope they are."

Jack nodded and went to the door with the agent and David. After waving good-bye, the professor returned to his desk and slowly shook his head. *A fine fix I'm in, spying on my daughter and son-in-law. Yet it must be solved. Could Daoud possibly be a member of ISIS involved in terrorist activity? He must be since he was the kidnapper. How could Louise so quickly be attached to him? When were they married, and how? How could she marry a Muslim? Did she join Islam?* Suddenly, Jack sighed and fell back in his chair. He remembered that his daughter had always said she wanted to marry a man of action, a man she could respect. He asked aloud, "Is he the man she dreamed of? What am I to do?"

David, evidently sensing that his master was in grief, put his head on Jack's knee and looked up at him knowingly and lovingly.

The professor patted the dog's head and said, "Let's go sleep on it," and they did.

The next day, Louise and Daoud, in great spirits, arrived in the middle of the morning.

Jack was amused and thought, *They must think they've got us all licked and will soon be on their merry way. I fear it will not be quite so easy.*

The three of them settled in the study with newspapers and coffee. There was a bit of tension in the air because they all knew that important matters were to be discussed, but who would start the conversation and make it seem natural and easy? Daoud preferred to avoid any verbal clashes, so he announced that he was going to play ball with David on the back lawn. He quickly left and enticed David with him.

With the air somewhat cleared, Jack said, "Louise, one thing that's been bothering me since our talk yesterday is in regard to your acceptance of Islam. How do you explain your ability to make such a radical change so quickly?"

"Dad, that's very easy to explain. You and I were hardly steadfast

Christians. *N'est-ce pas*? How often did I hear you say that if you called on God, you would not know whether to turn to Jesus, Moses, Muhammad, or Krishna? We always rallied around the group of them, not accepting any particular one for our prayers. When we said the word *God*, we actually referred to all of them."

Jack nodded. "That's true, my dear. We were never really anything, although I seem to be finding out more about myself of late."

"What do you mean?"

"When I learned that you were lost, I called on God for help. I subconsciously said aloud, 'Christ Jesus, help me!'"

Louise had a rebuttal. "Yes, but you were reared a strict Christian. I was not."

Jack looked downward as if ashamed. "Yes, I did not rear you wisely. Perhaps Islam appealed to you at a special time."

Louise walked over to her father and put an arm around him. "Dad, faith did come to me at a special time. I was in love with Daoud and wanted to marry him. We discussed Islam until I had a clear picture of it in comparison with Christianity. I accepted his religion, and we were married. I have never been so happy in my life."

"What was it that appealed to you most in Islam?"

"The similarities between the great religions. You have Jesus; he has Muhammad. You read the Bible; he quotes the Koran. Jesus and Muhammad are both prophets of God. Finally, both religions have similar rituals. The fact that Islam accepts our Jesus as a prophet meant much to me."

The professor looked at his daughter and asked, "Did loving Daoud so overwhelm you that you could change your religion?"

"Yes, Dad, and now I have a confession. Daoud's love for me has changed me completely. I didn't know love until he and I came together. Being in his arms and serving his great need for expression have enriched my life tremendously."

Jack was a bit amused and looked away. He had never thought of his daughter as one of the modern-day young people for whom he had only disrespect. In his opinion, sex played too much a role and too early in their lives. Now an Arab's bedroom prowess had overwhelmed his daughter. He wanted to laugh. She had expressed sex so poetically. *Oh, how the young deceive themselves!* There seemed only one thing to do: accept the fact. He sat Louise down and changed the subject. "What kind of wedding ceremony did you have?"

"A splendid one!" Daoud called out, having heard the question when he came back from playing with David.

"Yes, Dad," Louise agreed. "Some of Daoud's companions arranged it."

Jack, at the mention of Daoud's companions, quickly asked, "Are these friends members of a club?"

Daoud said, "No, there's no club. They're just friends."

Jack said, "Was there an Islamic priest?"

Daoud answered abruptly, "Islam does not have priests or clergy. Any Muslim who understands Islamic tradition can officiate at a wedding."

"Then one of your club did the ceremony?"

Daoud showed his temper for the first time. "No! There is no club!"

Jack calmly murmured, "Pardon me."

Louise, frowning with displeasure, spoke up. "Oh, it was all done by tradition. Even a ritual called the *mehr*. Is that correct, Daoud?" He nodded, and she continued. "That is a monetary settlement for the bride, but of course, we deferred that until later. That is allowed, and the groom gives the bride a ring to signify the delay."

"But was there a ceremony?" Jack asked.

Daoud explained, "Yes, the bride and groom both recite the word *gabul* three times. Then they accept something sweet, perhaps dried fruit, and they are married."

"That's very simple," Jack said.

"Yes," Louise said. "Isn't that wonderful?"

"Then I suppose that one of the cell read from the Koran?"

Daoud again raised his voice. "There is no cell. What are you trying to prove? Are you working for the FBI?'"

Jack squinted as if offended, and Daoud apologized.

Louise's face showed her surprise. Her mouth fell open, and she stared in amazement at her husband. She had never seen him so upset before. He was gnashing his teeth. After a few seconds, she calmed down and walked over to Daoud, whom she embraced. Then she said, "Our *nikah*, which is the word for a marriage ceremony, was abbreviated because of the situation. Yet we were both very pleased and happy."

Daoud calmly agreed with her, and they sat down on a settee together.

Jack suddenly expounded on some theories he remembered from his research about Arabic ceremonial marriages. "As I remember, Syria was the first country to allow a man to revive the ancient custom of several wives."

"That is true," Daoud said, "but you need never worry about Louise and me. We would never want someone else in our lives."

Louise smiled and turned to her father. "See, Dad? We are so close we can't imagine such a thing."

Jack smiled and nodded, but a silent fear swept through his mind. He could not understand how his brilliant daughter could be so naive and trusting and so sure of something that would be years ahead.

Jack continued. "I also remember that you can divorce a wife just by saying, 'I divorce you,' three times."

Louise laughed. "Well, Dad, you need never worry about that. I'll put my hand over his mouth."

They all laughed. Jack was delighted to hear the joyous voice of his daughter when she was witty, and Daoud gave his wife a hug and a kiss. Then he said, "No, we'll never part. We're stuck together forever."

The professor smiled, but the fear he felt was causing tension, so he excused himself and went to the bathroom. In order to keep the pleasant atmosphere in the room, he said as he walked away, "Old age for men is nothing but one short trip after another." He pointed toward the bathroom, and they all laughed again.

Shortly afterward, Mr. Fermel appeared, and the day's visit was over. When he came into the house, he said, "I thought I heard laughter when I came up the walk."

"You did," Louise said. "We've never been so happy."

"That's fine," the agent said. Then he apologized for having to take the young couple back to their quarters. As they were leaving, Mr. Fermel had a chance to whisper to Jack, "I'll phone you from my office."

The professor immediately went to his study and waited for the call. It soon came, and Jack said, "Today, for the first time, I was able to suggest that Daoud was part of a cell. It immediately brought on the first show of temper that I have seen. He denied it twice. I first used the word *club*, which upset him, but when I said *cell*, he simply exploded. I could tell by Louise's reaction that it was the first time she had seen him away from the role he was playing."

"I see that you also believe he's hiding the truth from your daughter. I fear for her. I think she's in for a disturbing realization very soon."

"I don't want her to be hurt, but I do not see any other end to this situation. What will she do when she realizes that he is a fraud?"

"It's a serious matter. She could easily do something tragic, because she's still naive and believes in him completely."

"Tomorrow I'll see if we can bring in the word *cell* again."

"Your help and concern are very useful. Do talk about a cell."

"At one point, he asked me if I was working for you, Mr. Fermel."

"That's good. He's suspicious. I believe we're on the right track."

"So do I," Jack agreed. "Tomorrow I'll try again."

"Good luck, and good night, Professor."

Unable to sleep that night, Jack tossed and turned while he concentrated on a means of revealing Daoud's hypocrisy. Before sleeping, he concluded that the best way to encourage conversation with his son-in-law would be through their religions. Islam might have some things in common with Christianity, but there was also a world of difference. Jack decided to defend the faith of his childhood. It was, after all, the faith he had turned to during the recent trials put upon him by his daughter's disappearance and her faith in Islam.

At breakfast, Jack was drinking coffee when Mr. Fermel delivered the happy couple. Their smiles and kind greetings seemed artificial to the professor, but he was in a mood for a showdown with his son-in-law. He finally said, "You two are living these days like vagabonds, being escorted from one cell to another."

Daoud set his coffee cup down hard, as if it were bristly.

Louise spoke up at once and looked at her husband as if to reprimand him. "Daoud, what's wrong with you?"

Turning toward his wife, Daoud replied in a snarling tone, "I don't want your father to insinuate anymore that we were in a cell. You know what that indicates in the media today."

"Oh, excuse me." Jack immediately apologized. "I guess I used that word because I've heard it so often in the news about terrorists."

Daoud's fist hit the table hard, and he raised his voice to say, "But we are not terrorists. Can't you get that into your goofy head?"

"Daoud!" Louise called out. "Please! We are guests, and you know that no harm was meant by using that word."

"No, I don't know if harm was meant. Maybe it was meant. He wants us to confess something that just isn't true."

Louise put an arm around Daoud's shoulders and made a rebuttal. "I don't think so, darling. Father would not want to purposely offend us. I can tell how happy he is that this mess is soon to be cast aside."

"Well, I'm not sure," Daoud said while almost coughing. "I'm not sure."

The professor was finally able to interject. "Let us calm down, children. Remember that the famous Russian poet Tyutchev wrote that 'a thought spoken is a lie.'"

Daoud frowned. "What does that mean?"

"He was speaking about the absurdity of human speech. It is so limited and can never fully pervade exact meaning."

Daoud, showing that he didn't understand by making a huffing sound, said, "I'm not sure. It seems to me that you chose the very word you meant to."

Jack backed off before something abusive occurred. "If you feel I should apologize, I will gladly do it. We should not have rampant words among our family."

"Sure." Louise kindly and sweetly spoke out. "We are too content and happy for any such thing as that."

Daoud tried to carry on the argument, but Louise cut him off. "Daoud, darling, let's take a walk in the garden for a little while."

The tall, well-built Muslim nodded, and the young couple went out onto the patio.

Jack was left at the table, drinking coffee. He was now sure that Daoud was hiding something from him, and maybe his daughter was too. What should he do next? Finally, he thought of a way to open up some hidden facts.

When the couple came in after playing with David in the garden, the professor said to Louise, "My dear, I've been thinking of putting some information in the newspaper about your recent marriage. I'm sure the public would like to know something more than the rumors that are being spread about. Tell me—what was the name of the Muslim who stood with you as a witness at your wedding?"

"Why do you want to know that?" Daoud asked in a tone that suggested suspicion.

"Dad would like to put an announcement of our wedding in the local newspaper," Louise answered.

Daoud's face wrinkled grotesquely. "Why does such a thing have to be made?"

Jack replied, "It's common here to announce weddings of local citizens. Louise is highly admired. Many people know that she was to be valedictorian of her college class. It would even be good to have a picture of your wedding ceremony."

Daoud was suddenly so angry that he almost jumped out of his skin. He yelled, "No pictures!"

Jack and Louise looked at Daoud in amazement. In a calm voice, she said to her husband, "Why shouldn't we have our picture in the paper? I'd like for people to see my handsome husband."

Daoud sneered. "That's silly."

"Are you hiding something?" Jack asked.

Daoud went on a rampage. He threw a chair across the room and yelled at Louise in Arabic. Turning toward Jack, he shouted, "There he is again, accusing me of something! Always trying to cause me trouble!"

A look of consternation covered Louise's face. It seemed that Daoud was holding back something that she should know and understand.

The silence that prevailed for a few moments was broken when Jack asked, "Does the great religion of Islam allow domestic violence?"

"Yes, it does!" Daoud practically screamed. "If a wife misbehaves, she is punished—and rightly so! Don't worry; you'll never see it. I'll be taking Louise to Iran when the stupid FBI finishes persecuting us."

A look of shock flashed over Jack's face. He could hardly speak. He looked at his daughter with fear in his eyes and then gazed at Daoud. "What? You'll live in Iran?"

"Of course. Do you think I want my children to grow up in this obsessed country? Never! We'll leave very soon."

Louise stepped in front of Daoud and calmly said, "Daoud, you haven't told me this. I'm really greatly surprised."

"Why?" he barked at her. "Do you want to stay among these infidels? That would be apostasy for our children."

The professor leaned back in his chair and said, "You mean you've been planning on moving to Iran, and you have not discussed it with your wife?"

Daoud's eyes opened wide and looked with hatred at his father-in-law. "Why should I do that? She obeys me!"

"Usually, a couple discusses such a serious move together."

Daoud pointed a finger at Louise. "She lives under the auspices of sharia law. She is happy to do so. Just ask her!"

Jack looked at his daughter, who was showing distress, as if she did not know what to do or how to react. He asked, "Is that true?"

"Yes, it's true!" Daoud yelled, and he went out onto the patio in a huff.

"Dad, I'll have to go to Iran with him."

"Why?"

"Oh, Dad, I'm pregnant."

Jack was horrified. "Oh dear God, no!"

Calmly, Louise looked at her father and asked, "Which God did you appeal to, Dad?"

Chapter 3

After Louise revealed her pregnancy to her father, she left him and went out onto the patio to be with Daoud. Alone, Jack sat down and tried to understand everything that had been said in regard to Daoud's plan to take his family to Iran. "I must stop them!" Jack concluded, and he decided he would help with Mr. Fermel's investigation.

When the evening dusk began settling over the patio, Louise and Daoud came back into the study with David. They seemed in a pleasant mood, as they were teasing the dog and laughing about something. Jack asked, "What's so funny?"

"Oh, Dad, there was such a silly incident in our wedding ceremony. I don't think I told you, but it does make us laugh when we recall it."

Smiling, Jack asked, "What was it?"

"Well, we wanted to follow the dictates of the Koran pertaining to the marriage ceremony. Men are often separated from women during the occasion. However, there is a place in the proceedings where a couple shares a piece of sweet fruit. If the genders are not together, a male substitute called a *wili* acts for the bride."

Daoud and Louise both laughed when the word was said. "Why is that funny?" Jack asked.

Louise calmed down and replied, "Oh, Dad, you know what? A wili is in the ballet *Giselle*."

Jack shook his head.

"Dad, of course you know. If a swan dies while being a virgin, she becomes a wili. Don't you remember?"

"Yes, but you see, I've studied sharia law, and I cannot believe that Louise would be content to live under such stringent circumstances."

"What are you talking about?" Daoud asked, his voice growing stronger.

"Well, for instance, I understand that you, as a husband, have the right to beat your wife for insubordination. Is that true?"

Daoud laughed, but there was a strange tone in his voice. "Professor, you can't believe that I would ever harm Louise." He laughed again. "You are medieval! Today our imams can give some latitude to the interpretation of sharia law. Besides, what could Louise ever do that would make me want to beat her? Oh, that's ridiculous!"

"Very well, Daoud," Jack said, as if he were surrendering in an argument. "Louise has not complained about you, so I should not have any concern."

"Thank you, Professor," Daoud replied smugly. "Now, I suggest that we have dinner. Louise is going to prepare stuffed grape leaves."

At that moment, the front door flew open, and several FBI agents ran into the room, followed by Mr. Fermel. The chief agent called out, "Daoud Faisal, I arrest you on the charge of terrorism!"

The FBI had entered so quickly and purposefully that the host and his guests could only stand in amazement with their mouths open in surprise. Daoud yelled, "What?"

The lead agent said coldly, "Cuff his hands behind his back. And you, Professor, come with me into the study." Once there, he whispered, "We have proof now, and I'd like to know if you can add to it."

Jack nodded and whispered, "He's planning on leaving the country with her as soon as your investigation is finished."

"That we know. Have you heard about a friend named Amir?"

"Yes, he seems to be the leader of the cell."

"We'll talk later," Mr. Fermel said, and he walked back toward the dining area. When he entered, he was confronted by a raging and yelling Daoud.

"On what charge can you arrest me?" echoed about the room.

"Terrorism!"

Out of Daoud's mouth spilled a long, frightening peal of Arabic. When he realized he was speaking his native tongue, he switched with the same vehemence to English. "You'll rot in Hades before you can prove such a charge. I have not done anything, and you're—"

Mr. Fermel waved for Daoud to shut up and loudly proclaimed, "What about Amir?"

Daoud's face turned red from his anger, but he stopped yelling. Twisting as if trying to free himself, Daoud snarled at the agent, "He's innocent! What do you mean 'What about Amir?'"

Louise and Jack stood to the side of the room and watched the scene with numbness. She could not understand what was happening, and he was delighted that something was finally happening.

When Mr. Fermel asked two agents to search upstairs bedrooms, Louise accompanied them to the second floor. Daoud insisted that there was nothing up there for them to find and that he was going to have the Iranian Embassy investigate their searching.

Mr. Fermel paid no attention to Daoud's babbling and waved for Jack to go back to the study with him. The professor walked around behind a table to avoid being near Daoud, who yelled in Arabic at him.

Daoud changed to English and growled at his father–in–law, "Oh, so you're in on this too. You'll learn to regret that you helped these assassins!"

The remark amused Jack, but he feared that laughing would make things worse. However, a small smile appeared on his face, and that caused another outburst from Daoud. "You rat! Just wait till you see what I'll do with Louise! Her own father rats on us!"

At that moment, Louise came running down from the upstairs and said to Daoud, "Darling, where is the key to that closet, and why is it locked?"

"You idiot!" Daoud shouted at his wife. "Why do you want to show them that?"

Louise stepped back in fear. "But, Daoud, they want the key, and we've nothing to hide."

"Don't give them that key!"

Louise backed up against a wall and raised an arm over her eyes as if to protect herself. "Daoud," she kindly whispered, "what is wrong?"

"You'll find out."

Suddenly, an agent came from the bedroom upstairs and said to Fermel, "We jimmied the lock and found what you expected."

Daoud spat on the floor and called out, "You had no right to get into that closet!"

Mr. Fermel paid no attention to the abusive captive and said in a formal voice, "You have the right, as a United States citizen, to refuse to answer any questions."

Daoud spoke up with a huff and said, "Well, I have questions for you!"

Mr. Fermel replied, "We'll have your interrogation at headquarters." Then he motioned for the agents to return to their vehicles.

Jack asked Mr. Fermel if it was necessary for him and his daughter to go with them. The agent answered, "No," and Louise ran to her husband as he was being led out of the room.

"Darling!" Louise called out as she ran up and threw her arms around Daoud. "I want to go with you. I don't understand what's happening, and I want to go."

Mr. Fermel objected. "No, this isn't the time for you. I'll be interrogating you tomorrow or the next day. Please understand."

The professor rushed over and put his arms around his daughter, freeing her arms from the embrace of her husband. She began crying.

Daoud, in a loud voice, demanded, "You stay here!"

Louise stepped back with her father and threw a kiss as the men led Daoud away.

Jack sat Louise in a chair and followed the agents outside. When they opened the door for Daoud, Jack heard his son-in-law yell, "Amir!"

The professor assumed that Daoud's friend had also been arrested, and he moved closer to the vehicle, but he could hear nothing.

After the agents and their captives had driven away, the professor returned to his study for a conversation with Louise. He was deeply troubled by the fact that she would willingly return with Daoud to Iran. After sitting down across from his daughter, Jack asked, "Louise, do you really think that you could go shopping at a souk?"

"What is that?" she said.

"It's the meeting place of all social and commercial activity in an Iranian town. I remember it quite well in the villages I visited while doing research there."

"Well, if that's where I have to shop, then that's where I'll go to the market."

"Louise." Jack's voice quivered from his despair. "You have no idea what a souk is like. People from all walks of life and speaking many languages come together there and bargain and sell things like spices, vegetables, meat, and cloth. It's another world!"

"Then I shall just have to learn their ways. Daoud would help me in the beginning, I'm sure."

Jack continued his argument. "Can you hassle?"

"What do you mean?"

"Can you quarrel over the price of a piece of material? I think not. You've never done that in your life. We accept the cost of an object or a piece of fruit without question for the most part. In Iran, you would have to litigate or plead for everything you purchase."

"I'll meet people and go with friends to the market."

"You forget that you will have little social life. The Koran forbids a Muslim to make friends with Christians and Jews."

Louise was becoming tearful, and her voice pleaded for kindness. "Dad, please stop. I'll just have to learn. Daoud will help me."

"Muslim men are either dictatorial or autocratic. I can see that in Daoud's character."

"Oh, Dad, he's been so kind to me. Please, no more now!"

Jack stood and put his arm around his daughter. "All right, my dear. I'll quit harping. Let's have a fire and get cozy for a while."

Louise agreed and joined her father. They sat in chairs before the fireplace. After a while, Mr. Fermel phoned with some incredible news. While Daoud was seated with his friend in the backseat of the FBI van, they spoke Arabic. While the FBI agents could not understand them, they supposed that Amir and his friend were discussing their situation. That was not the case. Amir had broken out of his cuffs and was working on Daoud's. At a street corner in the city, Amir had suddenly yelled something in Arabic, and Daoud had hit his guard. In a flash, the two convicts had been out of the van and running up an alleyway. They had not been caught, and Mr. Fermel was calling to warn Jack and Louise that Daoud might try to return for her.

The professor thanked the agent and then revealed the news to Louise. They were immediately aghast. If Daoud came for her, would she go with him? If Daoud came for vengeance, what should Jack do? A horrible fear set in, and neither father nor daughter knew what to do.

"God be with us," Jack finally murmured.

"You're praying to your Christian God, Dad. To whom should I pray—Allah?"

"Oh, my darling, dearest daughter! What have I done to you?"

"No, Dad, the question really is what I have done to myself."

Shortly afterward, two FBI agents appeared at the door and told Jack and Louise that Mr. Fermel had sent them for a night watch in case there were problems with Daoud. Jack was greatly pleased and did everything he could to make the men comfortable.

Jack and Louise took refuge in her bedroom and discussed their fears and concerns. Louise was in a quandary about her need for action and understanding.

"Dad, I just don't know what to do. I'm so confused by it all. I feel as if I should be doing something to help Daoud, but I can't discern what it should be."

Jack sat down on Louise's bed and took her hand. "My darling daughter, your perplexity is understandable. You're facing things one could have never prepared for. There are so many factors to consider. What bothers you the most?"

"Dad, what should I do if he comes for me? I do not see how he could, but Daoud is very clever, and I would not be surprised if he showed up here."

"The guards would keep him away from us. There are two of them, and I'm sure they're well trained in such matters."

Louise was silent for a moment as she collected her thoughts. Then she turned to her father and asked, "Do you think I should tell him that I'm pregnant?"

"I don't think so. Besides, as I said, I don't think he will be able to get to you."

A frown came over Louise's face. "But if he does, what should I do? I do not want to go with him because of my baby. I couldn't run or however he would want me to go."

"Oh, Louise, you're acting delusional. Such a terrible situation is not likely to take place. Don't imagine such things."

"I can't help it. I know how strong he is, and I don't want to oppose him if he insists that I follow him. He could pull me along without realizing that I am weak and worried about my situation."

Professor Demonte paused before he said, "I don't think you need to worry about that. What's more troublesome to me is how you could adjust to life in Iran under sharia law."

"That's also on my mind continually. I'm not even sure that I can bow to Allah."

Jack put his arms around his daughter. "Oh, my dear, we must stop such suppositions. We really don't know what to expect."

Professor Demonte shared his daughter's fears and wondered if he should try to stop Daoud if he dared show up. How could Daoud possibly get into the house with two agents watching below? Should Jack shoot him if he overpowered the agents? Father and daughter had never faced such a dramatic situation, and neither knew what to do.

Again, the night was filled with strange sounds, which were actually nothing more than electrical and technical equipment performing their usual duties in a home. Nevertheless, Jack didn't leave Louise's side until after one o'clock in the morning.

About an hour later, an amazing event took place. Daoud entered Louise's bedroom and covered her mouth with one hand while holding a flashlight in the other. Startled, Louise squirmed until her husband flashed his torch on his own face for her recognition. She quit moving and whispered through his fingers, "How can you be here?"

"I've come for my wife. Amir has the agents tied up. We've got to hurry. Get dressed."

Shaking from fright, Louise slipped out of bed. While slipping into her panties, she wondered if she should call her father, but she decided it might be dangerous for all concerned. When she was almost dressed, a loud crash sounded from the first floor. Daoud ran into the hall and bumped into Jack as he ran out of his room. Daoud yelled in Arabic to Amir, who answered quickly, and then said to Jack, "Just a bumbling agent. Come downstairs with us."

The professor put his arm around his daughter, and they followed Daoud down the stairs and into the study. Amir came and discussed something in Arabic with his fellow escapee. Jack and Louise sat down on chairs by the desk. They noticed an agent on the floor, wriggling to free himself.

Daoud ran in and said to the agent, "We'll go now! A friend will be watching you. If you call the FBI, you'll be shot. Give us thirty minutes." Turning to Louise, Daoud said, "Are you ready?"

"She cannot go with you." Jack bravely spoke out and then coughed hard.

"Shut up! She's going! Come on!" He reached for Louise, but she backed away.

Jack nervously said, "She's not going. You cannot make her go."

Daoud hit Jack across the face and knocked him back in his chair. Louise screamed, and her husband pulled her to him and covered her mouth with his free hand.

Amir came into the room and said something in Arabic. Daoud yelled, "Just a minute!"

Jack jumped up and put an arm around Louise, who was caught in Daoud's arms. He tried pulling his daughter away, but she was tightly held. "Do you want to hurt her?" Daoud called out, his eyes flashing.

"No, I don't. But she doesn't want to go with you!"

Daoud lowered Louise and stood her before him, holding her tightly with both arms. "What do you want? Do you want to stay here?"

Louise was in no condition to make a decision. A thousand thoughts were flashing through her mind. She feared what was feasible. They would be caught, and she too would be a prisoner. Was she being illegally taken out of the country? She would then be under sharia law. She would be a sharia wife. She would be deserting her father. She could not appeal or complain in such a situation. She must think of her unborn child. Where would he be born?

Daoud started shaking Louise while yelling curses and threats. "You're my wife, and you do what I say! Remember?" The shaking continued until Louise slipped from his grasp and fell to the floor. Blood was flowing from her skirt.

Jack screamed. "She's hurt! You've killed your son!"

Daoud's face showed horror. "What?" he yelled.

An instant later, Amir ran in and shouted in Arabic. Seeing that Daoud was in a state of confusion, he stepped over Louise and pulled Daoud away from the scene. At Amir's insistence, the two men went out onto the patio. They had to leave and ran down the stairs into the darkness.

Jack left Louise on the floor and hastily grabbed the phone on his desk to call an ambulance. Going back to his daughter, he found her unconscious. Leaving her, he went to the FBI men, who were tied with catgut and taped to silence. Once Jack freed one of the men, he helped his colleague. The FBI was notified, and sounds of police vans soon filled the air.

When the ambulance came, Jack watched the porters carry out his daughter, and he accompanied them to the vehicle. Receiving permission to join them in the facility, Jack slipped in and sat holding Louise's hand all the way to the hospital. There, she was taken into the emergency room, and Jack was sent home in an auxiliary van.

Walking into his home, the professor thought only of one thing. *How can I ask God for help? Have I not abandoned the God of my youth? Have I not studied and written about all the many gods of mankind? Have I been faithful to any higher power?* His mind quit questioning, and he answered himself. *Yes, I have called on the God of my youth, and I have been helped.*

Jack went to his library and took the Holy Bible out of his desk. He sat down and looked at the book. Suddenly, he started praying. "Dear God in heaven, I ask your mercy for my wonderful Louise. I feel your strength in my asking. Have I finally found the meaning of life?"

Chapter 4

The next day, Mr. Fermel joined Jack, who was sitting in a lounge near Louise's room. "I have news for you, but first, I must ask how she is doing."

Jack bowed his head, showing his despair. "She's survived, of course, but we've lost the baby."

"Most unfortunate," the agent commented. "I'm sure she is most despondent." After Jack nodded, Mr. Fermel changed the subject. "There will be a grand jury."

After a short pause, Jack asked, "When will the grand jury meet?"

"Oh, that will take awhile. Nothing in the courts moves quickly. You'll find that out."

"Good," Jack responded. "That will allow her to heal and be ready for questioning."

"Certainly. And please know that we shall do everything we can to make the ordeal as easy as possible."

"Thank you," the professor said. "Would you like to see her?"

"If she wants company, I would like to tell her some news. I'm not sure she would want to be bothered now."

"She'd probably like to hear any news from you that pertains to Daoud."

"Let's go then."

The two men went into Louise's room and found her sitting up in her bed, anchored by pillows.

Jack sat down on the bed with his daughter. Mr. Fermel greeted her kindly before saying, "I have news for you."

"Oh, wonderful!" Louise said, smiling.

"It's rather serious stuff. Do you want such news now?"

"Please, Mr. Fermel! I am ready for anything you have to tell me about my husband."

"Daoud and Amir have been caught and arrested. They are now in a federal prison. Amir will be deported, and Daoud, as a US citizen, will face a grand jury. It will be a very complicated process."

When he finished talking, Louise asked, "Is Daoud well? I mean, he hasn't been harmed, has he?"

Mr. Fermel grinned. "No, he's fine and in a proper place."

"Oh, thank you," Louise earnestly said, carefully wiping her tearful eyes.

Jack said, "You will be well and strong by that time."

And it all came to pass. Amir was not given a chance to express his anti-American sentiments. He also confessed to being responsible for two matters that freed Daoud from guilt. He admitted that he had talked his partner into escaping from the FBI when they were being taken to imprisonment. He also maintained that he had succeeded in handcuffing the FBI agents who were guarding the Demonte house after he and Daoud escaped. When asked how he'd managed to tie up two guards, he related that he had grabbed the gun of one of the men and made the other man tie up his partner. Then he'd knocked out that agent and tied him up. Daoud had not participated. The court exiled Amir and sent him to Iran.

Daoud was assigned a federal lawyer, with whom he prepared his defense. The grand jury awaited its turn in the federal proceedings. Louise returned home a weak and saddened loser. She and her father daily prepared for her unwelcome participation in her husband's legal problems. The waiting intensified their concerns.

One cool fall day, Jack suggested to Louise at breakfast that they take a long walk before settling down with a fire in their fireplace. His daughter liked the idea, as she had been restoring her health through exercise for some time. Wearing sweaters and accompanied by David, who was delighted with the change in their routine, the family set out for their excursion through the hilly neighborhood.

Mrs. Logan called out a greeting when they left the house. She had kept a close watch on the family ever since the FBI had imprisoned Daoud. Jack and Louise waved to her and answered her "How are you?" with smiles and declarations of "Just fine!" They were glad that they had surprised her in her housecoat, which would hinder her from running after them. They were free to challenge the brisk morning air.

"Dad," Louise suddenly said as they turned a corner going uphill, "will I ever be the same?"

Jack smiled. "Not quite the same but a stronger and wiser person perhaps. I know that in my own life, I faced many turns in the road and usually took the wrong way. Still, I like to think that I learned from my mistakes, as painful as they may seem."

"That's nicely put, Dad, but I see only a dark alleyway ahead, and I can't tell which direction is the right or wrong way."

Jack stopped and looked at his daughter. "Yes, my dear, I understand. You are facing a delicate and difficult decision. I want to help you, but I can only tell you my desire, which might not be the right one now. One never knows."

"Dad, I feel as if I'm trapped between two worlds. I liked my life before I was married, but I also am very much in love with Daoud. Not his universe, you understand, but his milieu. You see, life with him when he was a loving husband was just wonderful. Perhaps I was terribly naive, but the strangeness of his sharia teachings seemed so intriguing and far away. I was simply captivated by him and the prospect of a happy life in his culture."

"Didn't you ever question him about the meetings with his friends in your apartment?"

"Yes, of course, but he always said that they were planning a new business under the Homeland Act, which would finance their importation of ceramics from the Middle East. It always sounded so proper, and I was always reminded that being a Muslim's wife, I should not interfere. So I didn't."

"Surely it must have seemed very strange?"

"Yes, it did, but everything about my life with him was strange. He was such a powerful force—alive, active, and positive. You really never knew him as I did. The man who confronted the FBI was a shock to me. I found myself as I feel now—between two worlds."

Jack walked ahead, leading Louise with him. "You feel that way because you have not yet chosen which path to take. A truly weighty crisis is ahead of you. I have found solace in the religion of my youth. As to whether that is for you, I do not know. I did not really raise you as I should have. I filled your head with all the gods of the world. Did I do enough for you in our Christian faith? I don't know."

"Dad, I went to Sunday school, I prayed throughout my childhood, and I still pray to God. However, I am burdened now with Allah, but I still love the beauty of our church. As you say, I have much to decide. However, you did not deny me the love of God that you have found again."

"Thank you, my dear!"

Father and daughter walked in silence until they returned to their nest, their hideaway, their home.

As the time for Daoud's grand jury approached, Mr. Fermel made several visits with the professor and his daughter. It became obvious that the agent had a special interest in the oncoming proceedings. It was the first time there had been a grand jury with so many complications pertaining to an American terrorist.

During one visit, Mr. Fermel asked Louise, "Do you feel ready to bear witness before the jury regarding your husband?"

"Oh yes! I think so. I'm even going to have the dark roots in my hair touched up before he sees me."

Mr. Fermel laughed.

Jack said, "And I'm going to take David to the veterinarian for his last required shot before the parade!"

All three laughed.

The grand jury was held in a large room in the city hall. Since it was open to the public, all the seats were filled. Twelve members were selected, including Dr. Glasner, a noted lawyer and friend of Professor

Demonte, and Dr. Parker, the dean of students at Loyola College. A director was chosen, and he proclaimed several rules that were to be followed in the proceeding. Mainly, the public would not be allowed to question any witness until after all the evidence was given. Any question put forward at that time must pertain to the evidence given.

He asked for questions, but there weren't any. The director then read the evidence against Mr. Daoud Faisal, who was charged with treasonable acts against the United States.

Jack and Louise sat with the witnesses, and the revelations presented about Daoud contained much information with which they were not familiar. Several times, father and daughter looked at each other quite astonished. Other witnesses lightly squirmed when materials pertaining to bombs were presented. It was a serious charge in total.

The first witness, Mrs. Louise Faisal, was called, and she graciously walked to the chair by the director's desk. After she was sworn in to the proceedings, the prosecutor began the questioning.

"Mrs. Faisal, were you kidnapped by Daoud Faisal while you were walking to your college?"

Expecting such a question, Louise immediately replied, "I would not call it kidnapping."

"What would you call it?"

Louise explained the incident in full detail without trying to use a particular word to describe it.

"You entered a car without knowing the inhabitants?"

"I wanted to help them, as they were asking for directions. I was in a hurry, as I was late in my usual routine."

"It seems odd that a young lady these days would enter a stranger's car, does it not?"

"Yes, I agree, but at the moment, I was quite overwhelmed by the graciousness and kindness of the gentleman with whom I was speaking."

"Still, you entered the car on your own volition?"

"Yes. He was holding my hand and helped me enter the backseat with him.

A slight rustle and muted laughter sounded among the visitors.

"You were not alarmed that the car did not stop and let you continue your usual routine, as you put it?"

"No, I wasn't afraid." Louise then explained all the details of the meeting with Daoud and the effect he had on her immediately. She went into as much detail as she could and ended with the announcement that she'd married Daoud and could not have been happier.

When the witness finished, the prosecutor asked again, "So you would not call the incident a kidnapping?"

"No, I would not."

Dr. Jack Demonte was the next witness. He spoke of his incumbent position. "Yes, I am obliged to speak against my son-in-law, Daoud Faisal. I regret it very much. Yet he has convinced me that he is capable of being a loving and caring husband for my daughter, Louise." Jack listed events and actions in the past that showed the depth of Daoud's concern. It was a positive presentation. Then he commented, "We all have complex personalities. Under duress, we are all capable of freeing anxieties that seem outside of our character but are inside. Such was true of Daoud. Reared in the milieu of two societies, the Islamic and the Christian, it is possible that the clash of two distinctive religions affected him in positive and devious ways. I believe his statement today will show this aspect of his character very well. Therefore, I shall not elucidate any negative concerns that I have about him. You can judge him after you know the truth."

Daoud Faisal was led into the large chamber in handcuffs, which were removed once he was in the chair of the accused. The prosecutor started with a question about his youth, and Daoud answered straightforwardly. He was reared in Iran until he was eight. His family moved to America, and in time, he became a citizen. At that point, the prosecutor asked an unusual question: "Mr. Faisal, having received the enviable education you had in Iran and America, would you please go into detail about the activities that have caused you to be accused a terrorist?"

"With pleasure," Daoud answered, and he turned around to the audience almost as a bow. "I love America as I love my wife." He turned toward Louise and smiled. She cast her eyes downward so as not to show tears. "Yet I do not want my children to grow up in a country that is so corrupt and racist."

A stir went through the audience, which quickly became quiet.

"No, I do not want them to suffer as I did because my skin is brown. Nor do I wish to live in this country where privilege is bought and corruption permeates the government."

A few visitors tried to applaud, but the noise died down immediately.

Daoud turned and smiled. Then he continued. "Nor would I feel safe in a land where a criminal can buy justice and avoid imprisonment. No, don't seek justice in America!"

Again, applause started but quickly ceased.

The prosecutor interrupted Daoud's splendid presentation and asked, "Mr. Daoud, how do you explain the dynamite and guns in your apartment and in your father-in-law's home?"

"Easily. Those materials did not belong to me."

"Yet they were in a closet in your bedroom."

"Yes, but they belonged to my friend Amir. He said that they were to carry out any orders from ISIS headquarters in Syria."

The audience muffled a few boos.

Mr. Faisal continued. "I admit that I have considered joining the ISIS caliphate that is sweeping the world free of the disgusting deterioration of human morality. However, I have never joined ISIS as a member, nor have I carried out any of its plans."

"What about your being in the car that picked up Louise Faisal?"

Daoud did not hesitate. "It was a practice run. I was standing in for a friend. It just so happened that the young lady was at the right place at the right time, and Amir decided we should do it immediately."

The prosecutor realized that the accused had revealed enough for an indictment, so he changed the tone of the session. "Mr. Faisal, if you were not indicted, what would you do?"

"I would take my wife and move to Iran, where my children would be protected from Western society."

The audience stifled several boos but was sympathetic for the most part. The prosecutor rested the case, and the prisoner smiled in the direction of his wife as they led him away.

Next to be called for questioning was Mrs. Logan, the neighborhood lady who had insisted that she had very important information to express. Her right as a citizen was accepted, and she marched her heavy frame up to the front of the panel as if she were modeling a new hat. After she took a seat at the end of the officials, the prosecutor asked, "Mrs. Logan, you are a neighbor of the Demonte family, correct?"

"Oh yes," she replied, pursing her large red lips as if she would be speaking most precisely.

"Do you have a pleasant relationship with the Demontes?"

"Heavens yes," she retorted. "Why, they hardly do anything without telling me!"

Someone in the audience loudly whispered, "Or she'd ask!"

The slight giggle that resounded was quickly subdued, and the grand marshal announced that the hall would be cleared if any such disturbance took place.

Mrs. Logan sat too serenely to give notice to such an outburst.

"Now, Mrs. Logan," the prosecutor continued, "you mentioned in your interview for this jury that you had important information to relate in support of Louise Demonte."

"Yes, I do. I saw her leave her home the morning of the kidnapping."

"It has not been determined if there was a kidnapping, Mrs. Logan, so we shall not use that term with the grand jury."

"Well, I saw her leave her house."

"Did you see her enter a car?"

"No, that was too far up the block!"

"Then where is the importance of your statement?"

"I'm a witness that she left her home that morning."

A slight "Aw" suddenly hovered in the air of the large room.

The grand marshal hit the officials' table with his hand mallet and looked at the audience with a severe facial expression.

The prosecutor continued. "You mentioned seeing black-hooded men when you gave evidence for this council."

"No, I didn't actually see black-hooded men. I heard about them."

"From whom?"

"Oh, I don't remember. Evidently, many people did see them, as everyone was talking about them."

The "Aw" started again, but the prosecutor continued. "Perhaps not as many as you might believe. Actually, no one else reported seeing them. That will do, Mrs. Logan." He then showed great levity in thanking Mrs. Logan and allowed her to march back to her seat, which she did as if she were showing off a new hat and had been a star witness.

Jack thought, *We'll never be able to live with her now.*

The grand jury proceedings continued only long enough for a vote to be taken. Daoud was to face trial for his un-American activities.

After the close of the grand jury, Louise and Jack returned to their home, greatly depressed. The trial would not be for two months, and that meant that the disturbing things they had learned about Daoud would not be settled. They would have to hear them again at the federal proceedings against the indicted member of the family. Daoud's confession and his condemnation of his own country weighed heavily on his wife and father-in-law. His statements placed them in the position of deciding their own fate. How should they react to such vehement outbursts? Why hadn't Louise realized what was being discussed in those secret meetings of her husband and his friends? There were many questions awaiting answers. That was the cause of the downcast and humiliating despair they endured. They had no answers. They felt deserted and lost in a situation they had to endure and come to terms with somehow.

There was no straight line of inquiries in the hazy maze of matters that needed to be discussed, understood, and finalized. Her husband had been indicted in a frightening case involving treason. What should she do? If she again tried to support him, would her testimony be believable, since Daoud had considered pledging subservience to the ISIS caliphate? Also, if she was asked if she would go with her husband to Iran should he not be judged guilty, would she go? She did not know. There were so many factors that needed attention that Louise often found herself in tears and unable to discuss anything with her father. She felt embarrassed. Their wonderful rapport no longer seemed natural, and they usually left a question unanswered. Yet both looked forward to the trial in the hopes that it would be short-lived. Wearily, the family waited.

Louise investigated the local library's collection of books pertaining to teaching handicapped children. Since she might also teach an English course, she reviewed the fine aspects of English grammar. She did not realize that the subject was a matter of debate among American administrators. In her research, she found out that many believed that grammar studies were a waste of time and that oral expression was the better way to improve a student's English. She concluded that she would have to find out which approach was acceptable in any school in which she would be working.

Jack spent his time reading the Bible. He had with him at all times the Koran, the philosophies of the Far East, and the Talmud so that he could compare thoughts in each of the great religions. When his mind would wander to a poet he enjoyed, he would sometimes say aloud some lines he particularly liked. For instance, Paul Verlaine's poem written from prison was one of his favorites. It ended with the following:

What are you doing there?

Yes, what are you doing with your youth?

Then he would laugh out loud.

David saved Louise and Jack from much anxiety as they waited for the trial. It was as if the dog sensed that something was wrong and had been called upon to alleviate it. Each day, he insisted on a walk in the morning and in the afternoon. When he was fed, he always ate what was given, even though the cereal that was sometimes presented to him was not his favorite. He often put his head on their knees and looked pitifully at their faces until they petted or hugged him. Louise and Jack both agreed that David knew that something was happening, and he was trying to help.

Since visits with the indicted were allowed, Louise and Jack knew they had to face Daoud after his incredible confession. She had days of delay before visiting Daoud, because she could not answer her own questions. Finally, after the professor convinced his daughter that they could wait no longer, Louise agreed to meet with her husband. Jack called Mr. Fermel, who arranged for the family to confront each other. Louise insisted that her father be allowed to be with her during her talk with Daoud, and that was allowed.

Walking between the rows of cells in the federal prison seemed like visiting a movie set. Neither Louise nor Jack looked into the compartments as they walked down the passageway. At last, after what seemed like a mile of steps, they reached Daoud's sanctuary. He was standing at the front, holding on to the bars. Louise took one look and broke into tears. "Oh, Daoud! No!"

Jack put his arm around his daughter and greeted his son-in-law, saying, "Hello."

Daoud reached through the bars and pulled Louise to him. He pressed his face as close as he could to the steel bars so that he could kiss her. Her head turned, but an ear went through, and his lips touched it.

Louise stepped back, calmed herself, and said, "Thank you, Daoud. I love you."

"My darling, listen to me closely," Daoud whispered. "I ask only that you wait for me."

Louise started weeping again and raised a handkerchief to her face.

"Listen to me, darling," Daoud continued. "You are my wife, and I love you. We shall be happy again."

Jack spoke up. "Daoud, such terrible things were revealed at the grand jury. How could you have deceived us so mercilessly?"

"Jack, I regret that I had to involve you, but Louise is my wife, and she has to submit to my needs."

The professor adamantly and quickly said, "Maybe then, but not now!"

"What do you mean?" Daoud angrily called out with disgust. "She is forever my wife. We are one in the eyes of Allah!"

Louise lowered her handkerchief and said, "Daoud, you deceived me!"

"I had that right. You are my wife. It wasn't deceit; it was our relationship. You have no voice in certain things. That is the law of Allah. You are my vessel, which holds our love and devotion forever."

"But you never talked about such things. You never demeaned America to me!"

"I did not need to. As my wife, you were obliged to accept whatever I felt or believed in."

Jack again spoke out. "But you made my daughter an accessory to criminal acts by storing all that material in her bedroom."

"It was my bedroom too, and as my wife, she would naturally be involved with me in any sort of activity I would choose."

Louise spoke in a voice that appealed for understanding. "But, Daoud, you're an American as much as I am, and you know that what you are saying is not the way we associate with each other. A wife and husband share their problems and beliefs."

"But not a married Muslim couple! The wife is submissive to the dictates of her husband, and that is part of the sacred vow she takes with him in the name of Allah."

"I'm sure my daughter did not understand the severity or the extent of such a vow," Jack said, raising his voice a little.

"Of course she did!" Daoud yelled. "I went into great detail and outlined all the possible aspects of a Muslim marriage. She was fascinated and surrendered her heart to me before she took the holy vow."

Louise turned to her father and said, nodding, "Dad, he did. I listened to it all, but I was so in love I would have accepted anything."

"And you did," Jack said, also nodding.

Mr. Fermel, who had been listening close by, moved to them and broke into the conversation. "Excuse me, lady and gentlemen," he said while waving for another man to approach them. "I would like to introduce a federal lawyer who will participate in Mr. Faisal's defense.

May I introduce Mr. George Hamilton? He is one of our most astute legal authorities."

The family greeted the newcomer, and Daoud nodded without speaking. The guest immediately brought into the conversation a particular point that he wished to clear up in the evidence against Mr. Faisal. "One of the main points of importance has to do with the relationship between Mr. and Mrs. Faisal. If you don't mind, I'll call you by your first names."

No one objected.

"The prosecutor will undoubtedly try to indict Louise because of the overwhelming evidence uncovered in the apartment and in her home. It is very important then that we prove that she was not involved in any of the collecting of the materials or in the planning of what was to be done with them."

Daoud, in a loud voice, quickly said, "She knew nothing!"

"That is easy to say", Mr. Faisal commented, "but it must be backed up with something more substantial."

Before Mr. Hamilton could continue, Daoud spoke out, as if he had been waiting for such a question. "It must be pointed out that the status of a Muslim wife is different from that of a wife in the Western Hemisphere. Eastern customs play a great role in a Muslim marriage."

Mr. Hamilton, jotting down something in a handbook, broke in and said, "Excuse me, Mr. Faisal, but could you give an example?"

"Of course," Daoud said, as if he'd expected such an interruption. "It can be easily shown that a Muslim wife is subservient to her husband and not included in many aspects of the marriage. I am referring to the domestic economy and social activities."

"You have proven your point quite well, Mr. Faisal," the federal lawyer said. "Now let us turn to another point of value. It will be difficult to convince a jury that there wasn't a kidnapping."

Louise quickly came out of her standoffish and saddened state, saying, "There wasn't a kidnapping."

Mr. Hamilton said, "Why was a car with two masked men—"

A verbal explosion resounded at the mention of masks. Each

member of the family exclaimed almost in unison, "There were no masked men!"

Mr. Hamilton stepped back but showed that the outcry was amusing by a brief smile. "Excuse me. I was informed that the men were masked."

"That's the rumor that was circulated in the neighborhood, possibly by Mrs. Logan."

"Would you spell her name?" Mr. Hamilton said, and he jotted it down when Jack spelled it.

Continuing the conversation, the lawyer mentioned that the men driving down that street at that time could have easily known that Louise walked that route daily.

A discussion of Louise's acceptance of a ride by a perfect stranger went on for some time. At each break in the explanation of her behavior, the lawyer asked again, "Why did she enter the car of a complete stranger?"

Finally, Jack introduced an incident that reflected on Louise's conduct. It was well known in the family that Louise had done some absurd stunts in her life. She was supposed to go to the first dance she attended at her college with a friend of her close classmate Sally Smothers. While she waited for the ride, another young man drove up and talked her into going with him. She spent the evening with him instead of the designated guest.

Mr. Hamilton smiled and said, "A most touching story, but it's rather light. We'll have to concentrate on this aspect before the trial. We might have to ask Louise to take some psychological tests, if she wouldn't mind."

"I'd do anything to help my husband. Really," she said earnestly.

"Fine," Mr. Hamilton said. Then he added, "Now I must go. It's been a pleasure talking with you, and I can see that we'll work together most agreeably."

Everyone thanked the lawyer for coming, and all felt a sense of positive relief that they were in capable hands.

Yet the family was surprised the next day when Mr. Hamilton called and said he had arranged a meeting for Louise with a psychiatrist used by the FBI for such occasions. It was obvious that the behavior of Louise the morning of the so-called kidnapping was important in regard to the motive for Daoud driving down that street at that time. She agreed readily, and accompanied by her father, she went to the office of the physician.

During the extensive interview with Dr. Joseph Schwarz, Louise was told that her explanation of why she'd joined the stranger in the car was a major problem in the defense's approbation. In other words, it did not make sense. The question went through another discussion of possibilities, until finally, Louise said, "My fiancé and I were on the verge of breaking off our engagement. I was distraught."

Mr. Hamilton's mouth dropped open. "You have not mentioned that before. Is there a reason you have avoided such information?"

Louise shook her head.

"Will your fiancé testify to what you have just revealed?"

After a slight hesitation, Louise said, "Yes."

"This just might be the thing that can be used to vindicate your behavior. I will need to speak with your friend. What is his name?"

"Roger Hamstead."

"Will he cooperate with us?"

"I'm sure of it. I'll contact him immediately."

Roger met with Louise but said he preferred not to participate in the trial of a terrorist who had absconded with his fiancée. Louise was thrown off guard by Roger's reaction. She had taken it for granted that he would cooperate without the blink of an eye. While they'd had difficulties, she had actually thought he would be glad to be rid of someone who had left him so abruptly. Therefore, she interpreted his refusal as a means of vengeance.

"That's absurd," Roger said. "Shouldn't I be glad that you've shown yourself for what you are?"

The unkindness of his remark caused Louise to wince and ask, "And what kind am I?"

"You know! We talked about your haste in wanting to marry before I finished law school."

"But you remember how perfectly it would have worked out. I

would teach while you finished, and then we'd start building our lives together."

"Yes, you had it all planned."

"But, Roger, it was for us. Are you trying to tell me that you really didn't care for me all that time?"

Roger shook his head and said, "No, you know I loved you. Of course, we had some things to work out, but every couple does."

After a brief silence, Louise pleaded, "Roger, please help me now!"

Roger turned and looked in her eyes, which were tearful. Looking downward, he began his acquiescence. "I'll help you, but first, you must tell me how you took up with that guy so quickly."

Louise quickly went to her former fiancé and put her arms around him. "Oh, Roger, thank you." He patted her on the back, and she stepped away. "In regard to your question, I hardly know what to say. He was simply the hero I had long wished for. You've heard the evidence I gave. That's really the only way I can explain it. It happened so fast."

"Too fast!" Roger blurted out.

"Not really, Roger. You know how there were times when we didn't know what to do or say? We weren't being truthful with each other, so we remained silent. I sensed then that you needed someone who could help you with your career. I knew I wasn't the one. I have no interest in judicial affairs, and I do not understand how you felt I would boost your career."

"You'd be my wife and the daughter of a famous scholar."

"Yet I would be living a lie. In Daoud, I found the answer to my daydream, and I succumbed immediately."

After a pause, Roger asked, "Do you regret it?"

"I would lie to you if I said I did. I cannot do that. I still feel close to you, and I regret that I treated you as I did, but I fell in love with a wonderful guy. His deceit has hurt me greatly. That's all I can say."

Roger met with Mr. Hamilton and said that he and Louise had been having problems at the time and that he could understand how she would have been carried away with the attentions of Daoud. She had wanted to marry and have a family, while he did not want such an arrangement until after he finished law school. Therefore, she'd given in to the attentions of a savior, in a sense.

Roger's visit to the psychiatrist gave the results that Mr. Hamilton had wanted, and he presented his overall defense of Daoud to the FBI in preparation for the trial. Again, Louise and Jack were faced with a lengthy wait before the decisive litigation that would affect their lives forever.

At home, Louise and Jack settled back into their usual routines. David again played a role in their feeling of security and companionship. Louise was awarded her bachelor's degree, though she asked to be excused from delivering the valedictory address. She did not want to be a news spectacle because of her private life. Since Daoud would probably be given a prison sentence, she applied to teach in a nearby high school. Since the fall schedule was soon to start, the faculty for the institution was already complete. However, since she was qualified to teach English and world literature and her father was a well-known scholar, they offered her a part-time position as an English teacher of delinquent students. She would also substitute for other teachers when they were absent. Louise accepted readily, as she felt qualified for it, and it would mean not thinking about some of the complexities in her life.

At her next prison visit, Louise told Daoud about her teaching assignment, and he immediately misinterpreted her plan. "They want to take you away from me!" he snarled, raising his voice.

"Daoud, that's ridiculous!" she exclaimed. "It's just something for me to do while I am waiting for you to be freed."

He laughed but replied in a calmer voice, "As if they will."

"Well, we can hope they do," Louise said in a softer voice, as if she wanted to show the weight under which she was living. "I live on the hope that we'll be together soon."

"If I'm freed, we're off to Iran. Remember that," he adamantly blurted out.

"Let's decide that when we know—"

Daoud interrupted her and said, "Just remember that we are leaving as soon as we can."

Louise smiled as if she understood, but she was afraid to say anything about such a plan. The possibility of his being freed was remote, and she was preparing for a prison sentence. She realized they would probably have years of waiting before any chance of leaving the country. Whether to go or not would be answered in the future, not at the present, so for the sake of harmony, she smiled again when he reminded her of their upcoming departure.

Jack usually accompanied Louise when his daughter went to the prison. He would allow the young couple time to talk and then join them. Daoud enjoyed talking with Jack, because he would bring news of current events and any information pertaining to the trial. So continued the wait.

The first proceedings of the trial, the arraignment, occurred earlier than anticipated. Louise and Jack appeared in a federal courtroom, where Daoud, handcuffed, was waiting with Mr. Hamilton. The prosecutors had already turned over the bulk of their unclassified evidence against the defendant, who was charged with conspiring to kill Americans. Judge Harry Kaplan explained to Daoud his rights as an American citizen and approved Mr. Hamilton as the defendant's defense lawyer.

At that point, Judge Kaplan explained that the rules for federal criminal trials provided the courts a great deal of flexibility, and narrow statutory renovations had been developed to deal with novel problems as they arose. Mr. Kaplan then looked at the defendant and said, "This flexibility certainly applies to your case, which has several novel problems that have not been previously judged in a federal court. I refer to your marriage under sharia law, which excludes your wife from an indictment. There is also the matter of testimony taken from your compatriot Amir that can be introduced, but it is not sufficient to support a finding that the evidence is what the government claims."

The judge looked around at the few people present and continued to speak as if directing his words to the defendant. "The purpose of this trial is to decide whether the government can prove beyond a reasonable doubt the truth of the charges against the accused." When the judge stopped and looked at Daoud, Daoud nodded to Mr. Kaplan as if he understood. The judge then explained, "In such cases as Mr. Daoud's, where there are so many circumstances to be considered concerning the approval of the evidence, the government proposes a bench trial instead of a jury trial."

Mr. Hamilton immediately stood up and said in full voice, "Your Honor, I am sure that the defendant would be willing to accept a bench trial."

Daoud blurted out, "What's that?"

Mr. Hamilton softened his voice and said, "The judge himself will be the deciding factor in your case."

"Is that good or bad?" Daoud suspiciously asked with a frown.

"I advise you to accept. It's much better for you."

"All right," Daoud muttered.

Mr. Kaplan then explained that he had received all evidence of a negative nature as well as the supporting evidence. He then read the charges against Daoud, to which, under Mr. Hamilton's direction, Daoud entered the plea of not guilty. Then the judge outlined the presentence investigation.

Addressing the lawyer and the prisoner, Mr. Kaplan said that before a sentence would be made, a probation officer would conduct a background investigation. "The officer will study any aggravating and mitigating factors present in the case and prepare what is called a victim impact statement. This particular part of the investigation is limited because the wife of the defendant, Louise Faisal, has sworn under oath that she is not a victim. However, she will be questioned about the offender's prior criminal record, personal characteristics, financial condition, social history, and circumstances affecting his behavior. Lastly, she will be asked for any information pertinent to the effect of the crime on the victim."

Mr. Kaplan looked at Mrs. Faisal and asked if she would be willing to talk with the probation officer and complete a victim impact statement, which would be presented to the court and made a part of the record at sentencing. Louise, of course, agreed.

"When we meet for the sentencing," Mr. Kaplan continued, "both parties may make a statement before a sentence is imposed." He then ordered the prisoner's continued detention and dismissed the court.

Daoud, in handcuffs, led by a policeman, nodded to Louise as they left the courtroom. She waved to him. The whole process had only taken twenty minutes, and Mr. Hamilton was pleased. As they drove to the Demonte residence, he explained that the affair had become rather simplistic. The laws that pertained to their situation could not be accurately interpreted, because there had not been the crime of kidnapping, since Louise had denied that a kidnapping took place. Looking at Louise, the lawyer said, "That's why you will be asked to fill out a victim impact statement. It's a bit odd since you claim you are not a victim, yet by filling out the form, you will close the matter forever."

"Thank goodness," she whispered.

"Then there's the terrorist matter. Since no intent for terrorist activity was disclosed and the materials stored in two places for such activity were the property of Daoud's friend Amir, the defendant's impact statement will clear that accusation. The trial for sentencing should be quite short."

"Thank goodness," Jack said, and they all laughed.

After dropping Mr. Hamilton at the FBI headquarters, the Demontes went home, feeling very pleased. David met them at their door, and he sensed the family's joy. What better excuse was there for jumping and barking?

Chapter 5

Once again, Louise and Jack settled into their usual routines at home while waiting for the sentencing trial to be called. David entertained his master while Jack started research on another paper. Louise kept herself busy doing several things. She read her favorite books, especially the poems of Verlaine and history, especially about the middle east. She rearranged the furniture on the patio several times, never quite sure if the shady area was kept clear. She also baked pastries from her mother's old cook book. All her activities tied her close to home where she wanted to be with David and her father. However, she did visit Daoud in the detention center but stayed only briefly so that he would not be given a chance to start screaming about their future in Iran. She was afraid he might endanger their case with his eagerness to spread the dictates of ISIS thought.

One evening, when Louise returned from a visit with Daoud, she heard Jack laughing when she entered the house. She went into his study and asked, "What's so funny?"

"Oh, good evening, my dear! Excuse me, but I was enjoying a laugh at your expense."

"What do you mean?"

"I happened to read about a dish that Iranians love and wondered if you'd be able to prepare it." He stopped and looked at his daughter and laughed again.

"What is it?"

"It's a mixture of pomegranate puree and ground goat."

"What's so funny about that?"

Smiling, Jack continued. "Well, I've never seen you make such a puree, nor can I imagine you preparing goat."

"I would learn," Louise answered abruptly.

"Now, don't get upset. I was actually thinking of your going to the souk to buy the produce you'd need."

"Is that funny too?"

"Have you ever bargained for—" Jack stopped and then calmly said, "Louise, forgive me, but it seemed funny when I first thought of it."

His daughter sat down, smiled, and said, "Dad, I'll probably lose my mind trying to shop and cook. I'll have to remember to send you examples of my kitchen tragedies."

"Oh, so you do think about your life there?"

"Yes, and I'd rather not talk about it."

"Sure, darling."

"I've been visiting the school where I might do some teaching if Daoud receives a negative sentence. I'd rather think about that now. The few hours I would help remedial students could divert my attention from the trial."

"Certainly, darling."

Louise also intended to study Islamic history. If she was going to live in an alien culture, she wanted to know its history. She asked Jack for help in reviewing the medieval past in the Middle East. He was delighted. Such mental activity kept her from considering the enormous question in her life: Should she go to Iran with Daoud or divorce him and stay at home? The legal papers for the trial also needed her attention.

Louise had two visits with Mr. Hamilton, who was completing the required background investigation that would obtain any information that might be helpful to the judge. Louise completed a victim impact statement, in which she again denied being a victim. Mr. Hamilton thought the situation was amusing. The victim was not a victim, and the criminal in detention was not a proven terrorist. The evidence from the searches was claimed to be circumstantial rather than incriminating. Only one major matter in the history of the proceedings stood out as problematic: the subject of intent, which was not readily discernable from the evidence but was evident in supposition. Daoud had declared himself a terrorist, and Louise had married a responsible Muslim. Mr. Hamilton concluded that he was glad he himself did not have to make the judgment for sentencing.

One evening, as a diversion from their usual discussion of the trial, Jack suggested they talk about Middle Eastern history. "I noticed you reading one of my history books," he said to Louise. "Shall we discuss some aspects about which you might have questions?"

"Yes, Dad. I found it interesting that the word *Saracen* became synonymous with *Muslim* and *Islam* in that early period."

"Yes, in the seventh century, Muhammad began the expansion of Arab power along the Arabian Peninsula. That movement was along the Saracen borderline, and the words became synonymous."

"Reading about the Crusades, I found that there are four time periods associated with the growth of each."

"Yes, but those time periods are artificial. Historians divided the Crusades so they would be more unified or, one might say, easier to handle. It was not a perfect system, as there was much overlapping."

Louise moved over by her father and continued. "From what I've read so far, the first crusaders were horrible. Why did Christian knights capture the city of Antioch and kill the inhabitants? They were Christians! The savagery and mercilessness of their slaughter is frightening to read!"

"They wanted to unite the Eastern and Western divisions of the church. Remember that many historians feel that Rome and Constantinople should never have been separated. It's still debated."

"Well, I shall read about the next time period, and we'll talk again."

"You're off to a good start. I might add to your knowledge that in the first period, four primary crusader states were created: the kingdom of Jerusalem, the county of Edessa, the principality of Antioch, and county of Tripoli."

Louise laughed. "Well, what a wonderful memory you have. However, if I ever want to mention them, I'll have you repeat the list."

Jack also laughed. "Well, you will see how the history of the crusaders wanders back and forth among the various crusader states."

"Thanks, Dad. Now will you have a hot toddy?"

"No, I'm off to bed."

Later that evening, when Louise was going to her bedroom after watching a TV documentary, she passed her father's bedroom and noticed that he was beside his bed in prayer. This was startling. Never in her life had she been taught to pray at the side of her bed at night. Prayer was part of her life, but she had been taught to trust God's mercy in her life, not to call upon the Higher Power for the trivia of life. Christ was not the man next door.

When Jack rose from his prayer, he went to Louise's room and said, "I heard you behind me. Did I surprise you?"

"You did, Dad, but I was glad for you."

Jack entered the room and sat down on his daughter's bed. "My dear, I would like to say a few things that have come to my mind during the trial. Do you mind?"

"Oh, Dad, I would be very happy to talk with you."

"Thank you, my dear. I have had much time to think about the great question that has been with me most of my life. You know it well: What is the meaning of life?"

"Yes, Dad, we have discussed your question in many   of   the world's religions and cults. It always seemed to me that there were the same conclusions in all of them: peace on Earth and goodwill to mankind."

"I think you understood it all very well, my dear, but I fear that mankind is not ready for only one religion. Your own situation shows the great divide that exists between the faith you have been asked to accept and the faith in which you were reared."

"Yes, I tremble to think of it."

"Then I shall tell you why I am on my knees praying for you."

"Dad, thank you so much."

"My conclusion after spending my life studying the holy faiths of all mankind is that the religion in which you are reared is the one that can give you more meaning than any of the others. It is something that belongs to the real nature of being, in opposition to the extrinsic. It is, in other words, intrinsic. It is part of us. I see now that it is not the religion that matters; it's the faith that all people have in support of the righteousness evident in all theologies. Therefore, I pray to our Christian God, and I feel better for it. Have I really reached the meaning of life that I searched so long for?"

"Perhaps you have, Dad. Now in prayer, you are concentrating on the ramifications of your belief. You see that in prayer, you can now find guidance."

"Thank you for that, my dear," Jack softly whispered to his child, and after a pause, he said, "Let's say good night."

Father and daughter both had just retired, when the phone rang. Jack answered and heard some unexpected news. Daoud's family had visited their son in prison and then talked with Mr. Hamilton about the prisoner. "I was amazed that they wanted a chat with me," Mr. Hamilton said, "but I am glad I visited with them. The parents are very conscientious people and are truly devout Muslims. They are most regretful that their son has denounced his good life in America, and they maintain that it was the friend named Amir who was responsible for Daoud's behavior. They asked for permission to visit him and Louise. I am calling to inquire if you both will receive them."

"We will be very glad to receive them," Jack replied. "When can that be arranged?"

"I assumed you would be willing and took it upon myself to invite them to your home today. Was I too hasty?"

"Not at all. They might be a great help."

"I'm sure you're correct. I shall bring them at ten o'clock to your home."

Jack hung up the phone, greatly pleased. He could not sleep after such a call and went to Louise's room. She was glad that Daoud's family had finally appeared, and the father and daughter looked forward to the meeting the next morning.

Mr. and Mrs. Omar Faisal arrived with Mr. Hamilton, as planned. Daoud's father was a large man dressed in a Western business suit that seemed to fit his demeanor. His wife, Eve, was in native Muslim dress and seemed reluctant to converse. She stood sort of behind her husband when they entered the house.

Jack graciously welcomed the Faisals, and they all settled in the study for a visit. There was no need for extraneous words or explanations. Both sides knew the problems and the situation. Mr. Faisal set the direction of the conversation.

"Professor and Louise," he said directly, looking at them, "we regret that we did not come to see you earlier, but we Muslims are under attack here in America, and we want to prove to all that we are loyal and steadfast Americans. It will take time, but we have a strong faith and believe we will be accepted eventually."

"Certainly," Jack said, and Louise nodded.

"Our son, Daoud," the father continued, "has misbehaved badly, and we are greatly depressed by his actions and situation. We want you to know that we will help you in any way possible. We would like to make it clear from the beginning that Daoud was never anxious to be with ISIS. It was his friend Amir who misled him."

Jack and Louise both thanked Mr. Faisal. Mr. Hamilton then stated that the couple had already made supporting statements with the court. They were planning that day to visit their son in detention. After their visit, they hoped he would be a more cooperative person.

Mr. Hamilton, always in a rush, interrupted by saying, "Yes, Louise, I shall take them now to visit with Daoud. I too hope your next visit will be pleasant."

Mr. Faisal shook hands with Jack and Louise and started out of the house. Mrs. Faisal lingered for a few moments and then went to Louise. "My dear, I fear my son has harmed you. I pray that all will be well, and you may come see me any time you wish."

Louise thanked the woman and squeezed her hand before she walked away.

Alone, Jack and Louise sat down and contemplated the ramifications of such a visit. How would it affect Daoud? Should

Louise visit with his mother? Was Amir the only influence on Daoud? Much more had to be learned.

That morning, Louise wanted a diversion from all the talk about Daoud and the trial, so as Miss Demonte, she went to the school for handicapped children and met the director, who had been absent when she previously visited. When she walked into the large brick building, a student in a wheelchair met her and welcomed her to the institution. Louise graciously spoke to the little girl and followed her as she went to the main office. There, the girl said good-bye to Louise and left.

Miss Bonnefield, the school secretary, left her desk and went into the hall for a chat with the newcomer. "We are so pleased to welcome you to our school. Even though you'll be with us just three hours two days a week, it will be a pleasure to have someone like you with us," the short, heavy young lady kindly said, and she motioned for Louise to follow her into the office. "I shall see if Dr. Halloway is busy now. He too wants to meet you."

Louise thanked her and looked around the office. There were all sorts of awards for excellence and many pictures of former students practicing gymnastics or outdoor sports. She thought of Daoud exercising in the detention center, where the facilities were kept in a haphazard way.

Before Louise could ask a question, Dr. Bill Halloway came out of his office directly toward the guest. He was muscular and handsome, with dark brown hair and eyes. His smile was contagious. "So at last, the school board has sent me some help. Let me tell you that we are more than pleased to have you join us. We hope we can make you enjoy our company as much as we are sure we'll enjoy yours."

Louise was somewhat taken aback by the long, pleasing outburst of the director of the program, but she thanked him kindly and followed him into a classroom, where he started explaining her duties.

"You see, Miss Demonte, we are handicapped ourselves, because we are actually forced to be two different types of educational facilities. We have specialized training for the truly handicapped, and we have a remedial school for those students who have failed in their classes in the high school itself."

"Are there so many who need extra help for their continued education?"

"Not so many, but enough to be a problem in the school. Your question shows me that you have seen the problem clearly. We receive young people with behavioral problems as well as remedial needs."

"That's quite a combination."

"Yes, it is, but it actually reflects the terrible condition of our educational institutions today. Like every organization today, we need funds. We need to build and purchase needed buildings and furnishings."

"It's always politics, isn't it?" Louise quipped.

"That's an astute remark," Mr. Halloway said, and they both laughed.

Walking over by a blackboard, the director continued. "I looked over the list of our incoming remedial students, and I believe you will be working with a few students who are greatly defunct in English, written and oral."

"That sounds interesting."

"We'll give you a desk and a small office, so you'll have privacy with the students. Some are embarrassed that they are remedial."

"Sir, I do have a question. It is personal. You do know that my husband is in detention and awaiting trial, don't you?"

Mr. Halloway stopped and kindly said, "Yes, we do, and it will not be mentioned here." He smiled and started walking away. "I'll talk with you again when school starts."

Louise thanked him kindly and went home, satisfied with the help she'd give the program.

At the next visit with Daoud, Louise was eager to find out two things: how the visit with his parents had gone and his reaction to her teaching in the remedial care program of the local high school.

Daoud did not like the idea. "No, you won't do that sort of thing. It's some kind of a trick to get info out of you."

"Daoud, that can't be true. The FBI doesn't care what I do with my free time. I thought you'd be glad that I can make a little money for us."

"We won't need it. When we are free, my family will help us."

Louise smiled and nodded. "I'm sure." Of course, she wasn't sure, but she dared not talk about the future, when it was so blurred at the present. "Look, darling—I've brought you some dates. I know how you like them, because they remind you of your childhood over there."

Daoud reached over the table and accepted the gift. "You're a wonderful wife, my darling. You've done everything I've asked of you." He smiled kindly at her as he opened the package and took out a date. "I'll never forget Mr. Hamilton's face when you said that you weren't kidnapped." Daoud laughed with a snide tone.

"Shhh," Louise whispered. "They might be listening."

Daoud's face turned red. "Don't ever shush me! A Muslim's wife doesn't do that to her husband."

Louise apologized, but she knew it was time to leave before he began raving about things that should not be overheard. She wanted to ask him about his parents' visit but decided he was not in the mood to talk about them. She took her leave after promising to return at her earliest convenience.

Driving home, Louise had a sudden sense of fear. *Is he really the man I should spend my life with? Did he not deceive me? Did I not lie for his sake, as I felt a wife should? Can I live under the dictates of sharia law? Do I want my children to be reared under the same restrictions? Oh dear God, what am I to do?*

Arriving home, Louise was greeted by David, but her father was away. She wandered about the house, walking slowly through the rooms as she thought of her situation. She wished she had asked Daoud about his parents; she would have liked to know their reaction to his behavior. Yet she knew she had been right to leave those questions for another time. She didn't want him to get upset while she visited. When she suddenly saw her father's history book of the Middle East, she sat down and tried to read so as not to think of her problems.

The Second Crusade was encouraged by the priest Bernard of

Clairvaux, but he was disgusted with the violence and slaughter he had promoted against the Jewish population of the Rhineland. She could see her father-in-law in armor on a large white horse. Louise put the book down and thought, *Such horrors all the time. What a ghastly history.*

She picked up the book and read aloud. "In 1187, Saladin united the enemies of the crusader states and vanquished the crusaders in savage fighting at the Battle of Hattin." Again, she lowered the book and pondered the text. *Nothing but frightful battles! Why didn't God help them? Why doesn't God help me?*

Louise dropped the book into her lap and thought, *Why did I call on the Christian God and not Allah? Am I not supposed to make the change? What would Daoud say? Do I care what he would say? Do I realize what I am saying? I do not care what Daoud would say!* Louise dropped the book, stood up, and walked out onto the patio. The fresh air revived her, and she looked at herself in one of the windows around her. "Well, Louise," she said aloud, "have you not made a discovery about yourself?"

When Jack returned home, Louise called him to the study. "Dad, what have I done?"

"What do you mean, my dear?" Jack asked as he took off his jacket and sat down across from her.

"I don't want to go to Iran!" Louise blurted out as she started to cry. "I don't know what I've done to my life or yours, but I know that I'm miserable."

Jack put his arm around his daughter and petted her back. "My dear, this is what I've been waiting for!"

Louise turned and looked at her father through her tears. "Really, Dad?"

Jack nodded. "You see, my dear, I did not believe you could adjust to sharia law. Your marriage would have been very difficult for you."

After a few sobs, Louise straightened up and said, "I know. I realized it at my last visit. I do not understand how I could have believed I could be a mate for Daoud."

"At first, I would say that it was the overwhelming excitement of such a change. Then, however, you began to doubt, but your pride would not let you admit it."

Louise turned and cried on her father's shoulder. After a few pats on her back, Jack asked, "Have you read more Islamic history?"

"The Crusades were so brutal. Both sides believed they were right and did horrible things in their righteousness."

"Yes, we humans are willing to sacrifice our moral principles when we are distracted by another moral code. Look what you've done! You are not a liar, yet you allowed yourself to be one in the name of Allah."

"Oh, Dad, what shall I do?"

"If you really want my advice, I'd say do nothing now. We must wait for the bench trial and find out what Daoud will be able to do."

"Yes, I'm sure you're right. Nothing now. Thanks, Dad." Louise broke away from her father and ran out onto the patio with David, who was jumping with joy, sensing that his mistress was no long unhappy.

That evening, Mr. Hamilton came with startling news. He was planning to file a motion to dismiss with the trial judge. Father and daughter crowded around their lawyer with questions about such a procedure. He pulled out a set of forms, already completed, from his briefcase and sat down at the desk in the study. Since the family could not stop questioning him, he finally said, "Let me do the talking."

Jack, Louise, and David became quiet and sat down around the desk.

"I believe we have a good case," Mr. Hamilton said, and he pointed to the form for the motion to dismiss. "In this section, I have pointed out that the court has no authority for such a trial. There is no guilty party, and there has been no crime."

Louise tried to say the same thing: "You've pointed this out before."

"Yes, but I did not ask for a dismissal. Look at this form. It shows that there is a lack of personal jurisdiction. That means that there is no authority on matters that affect one person. In this case, that would be Amir, whom they sent off to Iran because they had no jurisdiction over him."

"Thank goodness he left," Jack whispered.

"Yes," Mr. Hamilton replied. "Now look at this final form referring to the improper venue. Since it turned out not to be a criminal case, it is in the wrong court."

Jack asked, "Does this mean that Daoud will be released at once?"

"That is likely. In case he is released, I want you to know that his family has asked that he be turned over to them."

"Oh!" Louise exclaimed. "He'll want to go to Iran. Oh no!"

Mr. Hamilton's eyes opened wide at Louise's remark, and he asked, "Have you changed your mind about being Mrs. Faisal?"

Jack answered. "I believe she has. It is an answer to my prayers."

Louise turned to Mr. Hamilton. "He is not the man I married. I hardly recognize him now."

"This is very serious," Mr. Hamilton said. "It could cause many changes in the mind of the judge. I must think about the consequences if you divorce him."

Jack spoke up again. "In sharia law, it is the man who obtains the divorce, as I remember. In fact, all he has to do is repeat three times 'I divorce you.'"

After a long pause, Mr. Hamilton softly said, "The denouement of this drama must play out by itself. I fear that we must wait until the judge has ruled on this dismissal. Then we can confront the situation you will be in."

"Certainly," Jack said.

"Yes, of course," Louise added. "We'll tell no one that I've changed my mind."

Mr. Hamilton stood and put his papers back in his briefcase. "Let's not discuss anything now. Let's just pretend that we haven't broached the subject yet. We'll wait until we hear from the court."

All agreed, and David wagged his tail while escorting Mr. Hamilton to the front door.

Louise and Jack embraced. Both were tearful, but they did not have to say a thing. Both knew they might face a firestorm once

Daoud was free. Yet the situation might be calmer than they thought if he was released to his family. Either way, it was a confrontation of sorts that they would have to accept.

Louise suddenly broke away from her father and said, "Dad, I'm going to visit Daoud." Jack looked surprised. "Yes, Dad, I must face him. I want to know how he reacts to me since his parents have been with him."

"That would be interesting. We'll spend a lot of time wondering about that if you don't go."

The next morning, Louise went to the detention center and confronted her husband. Daoud came to the visitors' center, looking gloomy. He saw her and sat down behind the screen in the middle of a visitors' table.

She greeted him kindly, but he didn't answer. Instead, he just looked at her. Finally, he bowed his head and said, "They've worked on you, haven't they?"

"What do you mean?" she asked.

"Our parents! That's what I mean. Yes, I know they talked with you and that you didn't object when you found out I would be released to them whenever I am freed. You also know that the lawyer has asked for the judge to throw our case out of court."

"Yes, I knew, and I pray that he will dismiss our case. Then we shall face our fate. Daoud, you surely don't think I would want to live with you after the way you deceived me. And what about our child, whom I lost because of your behavior? The romance we had in the beginning was torn out of my heart."

Daoud continued to look at the floor. Finally, he looked at Louise. "You are still very beautiful, and you are still my wife."

"Only under sharia law, which, as you know, is not recognized here in America. You have the power to divorce me at any time."

"Is that what you wish?"

"Not now. Let us wait until we find out the judge's decision."

Daoud held up a hand as if he wanted to say something. "Amir, my friend, is arrested and in prison. I do not know all the facts, but I know that I'd be with him if I had followed his plan. Now I no longer have any ISIS inclinations. I am an American. I want you to know that I've listened to my father and agree with him. Amir misled me, and I accepted the propaganda that he was spreading. Thanks to Allah, I did not go to Iran with him. He is out of my life forever."

"Oh, Daoud, that's wonderful news. Let us pray that the judge will free us from a trial."

"You speak of prayer. To which God do you pray—yours or Allah?"

Louise smiled at her husband. "Daoud, my father has set an example for me. He concludes that a person finds surety in the faith he or she was reared in from birth. It is a matter of the heart. I feel that now, and I am so glad. I would not want you to change to my faith, because yours is also a great religion."

"I like what you are saying, and there's something I want you to know about me. My parents have visited me and have made me realize much that I had lost in my friendship with Amir. I am really now an American and have restored my faith in Allah. We both seem to have come to a similar conclusion. I think we'll have much to discuss after we know our fate."

"Yes, Daoud, and we shall, but please tell me how your parents helped you revive your faith."

"My parents have redirected me. I had become completely under the influence of my friend Amir. My mother and father had given up on me. However, when they came to the prison, they proved that they had forgiven me and wished to help me revive myself through Allah. I started with prayer and have been doing it five times a day. Allah has returned my respect for my parents and restored my faith."

"That's wonderful."

"And I also practice *wudu*, which is sort of like Christians' baptism. That is, by using the purity of water, one frees one's soul. I take water into my mouth and even inhale it through my nose. It's sort of a short ceremony. There are other aspects, and I am slowly accepting them."

"Oh, Daoud, I'm so happy for you."

"Yes, I feel better about myself too. I know it's making me a better Muslim. I even want to go to Mecca someday."

"I love you, Daoud," Louise tearfully whispered, putting her hands across the table for him to take hold.

"And I love you," he whispered.

Louise left with tears in her eyes, and Daoud stayed at the table until she was out of sight. Then he turned to Allah for guidance.

It came to pass that the judge did dismiss the trial. Louise and Daoud were free to face their fate. Their parents arranged for the couple to meet in the clubhouse of the city park. Dr. Demonte escorted Louise, and Mr. and Mrs. Faisal brought Daoud. The young couple came together and held hands as they turned toward the large glass doors of the patio.

"This isn't good-bye, Daoud," whispered Louise.

"No, it cannot be," he replied, lightly squeezing her arms.

Out in the park, they embraced while their parents waited inside the club. The couple walked out into a large garden, along a brick path toward woods. What they discussed could not be heard. It must have been much of what they had previously said to each other. Louise expressed her love for her Christian religion, and Daoud expressed his love for the Islamic Allah. As to whether the two would ever meet again, no one could know. Yet they embraced before the path diverged. Louise went to a distant Christian cathedral, and Daoud went to a distant mosque.

Printed in the United States
By Bookmasters